The Patchwork People

Keeper of the Universe
Andra
Calling B for Butterfly
Moonwind
Star Lord
The Warriors of Taan
Children of the Dust

The
Patchwork People

BY LOUISE LAWRENCE

Clarion Books/New York

Clarion Books
a Houghton Mifflin Company imprint
215 Park Avenue South, New York, NY 10003
Text copyright © 1994 by Louise Lawrence

First published in 1994 under the title THE DISPOSSESSED
by The Bodley Head Children's Books,
Random House,
20 Vauxhall Bridge Road, London SW1V 2SA ENGLAND

Text is 11-point Janson

Printed in the USA

Library of Congress Cataloging-in-Publication Data

Lawrence, Louise, 1943–
    The patchwork people / by Louise Lawrence.
        p.   cm.
    "Published in 1994 under the title The dispossessed by
the Bodley Head Children's Books . . . London"—T.p. verso.
    Summary: In a dismal Wales of the future, with few jobs
and fewer resources, a group of destitute, jobless young
people becomes involved with a rich girl whose life is impoverished
in spite of her material comforts.
    ISBN 0-395-67892-7
    [1. Science fiction.   2. Wales—Fiction.]   I. Title.
PZ7.L4367Pat   1994
[Fic]—dc20
                                                    93-40830
                                                      CIP
                                                       AC

BP   10   9   8   7   6   5   4   3   2   1

To Julie Fallowfield

The Patchwork People

1

It was a cold December morning, a few days before
Christmas. The city had made an attempt. A decorated
Christmas tree stood outside the castle, and there were
strings of colored lights above High Street shops, and in the
main department store Santa's grotto catered to those who
were rich enough to pay. Animated elves and a team of
reindeer laden with dummy parcels pranced in the windows amid Styrofoam snow. Small children watched with
rounded eyes . . . until nine in the morning, when the electricity was switched off and everything stopped. The lights
went out.

"There's a waste of money," said Hugh.

"They could have provided every unemployed family
with a Christmas chicken for what all that frippery cost,"
said Dilys.

"Asking for trouble, aren't they?" said her brother Colin.

"It'll be coming," said Flutey.

"You can feel it already," said Dilys.

"In the air," said Hugh.

But he could not have described it. It was a mood, an atmosphere of menace. Something that existed in the minds of people, showed in their eyes, a brooding discontent. It was in him too, an unexpressed anger waiting to be released. A line of people, shabby and silent, waited outside the post office to cash their welfare checks. The amount was being reduced by ten ecu a week, and there would be no Christmas bonuses this year . . . the government had just announced it.

"Bastards!" said Hugh.

"We'd be better off without them," said Flutey.

"Without who?" asked Dilys.

"Politicians," said Colin.

"So-called democracy!" said Hugh. "The government of the many by the few for the benefit of the few. What have they ever done for the likes of us?"

"They'll be giving us ninety ecu a week when we're nineteen," said Dilys.

"Big deal," said Hugh.

They walked along Park Street, crossed among buses and bicycles, and headed for Central Station. No signs of Christmas here. Just women with shopping bags come for the Thursday market, gangs of unemployed youths loitering in the bus depot, and a man lying on the pavement . . . drunk, or drugged, or dying.

Hugh and Dilys paused.

"Maybe we ought to telephone . . . ?"

"You got a phone card, have you?"

"No," said Hugh.

"Nor have I."

"Emergencies are free," said Hugh.

"But ambulances aren't," said Dilys.

"Well, we can't just leave him," said Hugh.

"He's not our responsibility," said Dilys. "He's a vagrant, a down-and-out. And the Salvation Army will find him soon enough."

And Flutey called.

"If we want to catch the nine twelve, it's arriving now!"

Through glass doors they entered the station lobby. Pimps and prostitutes loitered in the shadows, and Colin set up his shoeshine box. Hugh and Dilys followed Flutey through the underpass. The train from Nottingham had already pulled in when they reached the platform, joining others who were already there, begging for money or offering their services.

"Carry your bags, sir?"

"Carry your bags, madam?"

"Got any leftover sandwiches?"

"Any drink cans you want to get rid of?"

"Any Styrofoam cups?"

"If you've finished reading that newspaper, mister . . . ?"

"If you no longer need that magazine . . . ?"

"Find you a taxi?"

"Show you the way to the bus depot?"

"Need a hotel?"

Clamoring and determined, they followed the passengers through the underpass. And in the foyer others were waiting.

"Spare us an ecu, lady?"

"Spare us a demi?"

"Want your shoes shining, sir?"

Security guards yelled at them.

3

"Clear off, you lot!"

And they vanished in various directions.

Until the next train arrived.

By midafternoon not many remained. Cold, and hunger, and the security guards, had driven them away. Only Hugh and Flutey lingered in the men's restroom, and outside the station entrance Colin waited with his shoeshine box. And somewhere Dilys was still scavenging for Styrofoam cups.

It had been quiet for almost half an hour . . . no arrivals, no departures, and the guards swilling tea in the station-master's office on the opposite platform. Then, one by one, the passengers began gathering. Connections came from Rhondda and Merthyr Tydfil, and there was a feeling of imminence. The security guards left the office, and a voice over the public address system announced the next train due to arrive.

It was an intercity express from London Paddington . . . an ancient steam locomotive splendidly repainted in colors of the Welsh Railway Company, black with a scarlet dragon on the side, hissing fire and steam, and belching clouds of sulfurous smoke.

"Cardiff! This is Cardiff. Change here for stations to Rhondda, Merthyr Tydfil, Rhymney, Barry Island and Penarth. . . ."

The noise of the engine drowned the announcer's voice.

Hugh and Flutey went into action.

"Carry your bags, sir?"

"Carry your bags, madam?"

"Carry your bags, miss?"

"No thank you," the girl said curtly.

Just for a moment Hugh noticed her . . . an English girl

4

wearing a scarlet coat and fashion boots zipped to the knee. Her suitcase had wheels, and was decorated with vacation stickers from foreign places. She swept past him towing it behind her, to be lost amid the crowd heading for the underpass. He forgot her immediately and tried again.

"Carry your bags, sir?"

"Find you a taxi, madam?"

He had no luck with anyone, and neither did Flutey. Slowly the platform emptied of people and the train doors slammed shut.

The security guards vanished down the underpass.

"We may as well push off," said Hugh.

"Or wait for the three thirty from Rhymney?" said Flutey.

"What's the point?" asked Hugh. "Who comes from the valleys seldom has money for handouts."

"I'll go and find Dilys then," said Flutey.

"Right," said Hugh. "You check the ladies' waiting room and I'll try the cafeteria."

He thrust his hands in his parka pockets. There were holes in both of them. And his sweater had shrunk from too much washing. He could feel the chill of his fingers on the warmth of his own flesh. And the train pulled away. Smoke and soot, carried by the wind along the platform, obscured his view. But going through the underpass he caught a glimpse of scarlet.

The girl was standing outside the entrance on the edge of the forecourt, her suitcase at her feet. Her boot heels stamped restlessly from cold or impatience, and the wind tugged at the fair strands of her hair. Beyond her, in the bus depot, the orange city buses came and went, and half a dozen taxis drove away along the approach road. But the girl remained. Waiting, thought Hugh, for someone who had failed to arrive. And she was asking for trouble.

He approached silently on worn-out sneakers, watched her from a vandalized telephone booth, then lingered by the ticket machines pretending to be absorbed. A single fare from Paddington cost 500 ecu . . . she had to be loaded if she had made that trip. He pressed the buttons hopefully, but the machines gave no change. Drafts from a broken door whistled around his ankles, rustled the debris of travelers' fare: cellophane sandwich wrappings, potato-chip bags, an empty burger box. Posters on the wall advised him not to have sex without a condom, or expose himself to the sun. Then, as he expected, a gang of youths came from the bus depot and homed in on the girl, hoping for easy pickings.

"Hello, darling."

"Fancy a good time, do you?"

"A trip around the city?"

"See the Christmas lights?"

"Fifty ecu and we'll escort you."

"Go away!" said the girl.

The youths laughed nastily.

"Pity to lose your nice looks, it would be."

"Or lose your nice blond hair."

"But give us fifty ecu and we'll protect you."

"Make sure you're not molested, see?"

"There are some nasty bastards hereabouts."

"Go away!" the girl repeated.

Again the youths laughed.

"A bit hoity-toity, aren't we?"

"Doesn't do to get uppity with the natives, miss."

"We're only trying to be friendly."

6

"What you need are some joy drops, darling."

"We can supply you."

"Fifty ecu for five."

"Now what do you say to that?"

"Go away!"

Nearby, guarding his shoeshine box, Colin watched and waited. And Hugh made his move, stepped from the gloom of the lobby and picked up the girl's case. Her blue eyes widened in alarm but there was no way he could reassure her. He could only hope she would cotton on fast enough and play along with him.

"I've telephoned your mother, Miss Alice. The car's got a flat tire. She says to wait in the cafeteria and she'll be here in half an hour." He took her arm, glanced over his shoulder and saw Dilys and Flutey behind him, then turned to face the group of youths. "Want something, do you?"

For a moment Hugh thought they would attack. But Colin came to join him, and a police car turned into the approach road, followed by a blue Mercedes. The youths shrugged and turned away. Hugh put down the girl's case and released her arm.

"Better wait inside," he told her.

"We'll look out for you," said Colin.

The girl regarded them.

Her eyes were colder than the weather.

And her voice was withering.

"For fifty ecu each, I suppose? Get stuffed! Both of you! And just for your information . . . my name's Helena, not Alice! And there's nothing wrong with the car . . . it's arriving right now!"

Hugh clicked his heels and tugged his forelock.

"Very well, Miss Helena, nice to have met you."

"Ungrateful cow!" Dilys said loudly.

■ ■ ■

Helena opened the car door.

"You're late!"

"Sir Gerald Fraser telephoned just as I was leaving," said her mother.

"I could have been mugged, or raped, or anything!"

She dumped her luggage on the backseat, sat in front and fastened her safety belt. The car had darkened windows made of toughened glass to preserve their anonymity and protect them from attack.

"It was awful!" said Helena. "You've no idea how awful it was. I was all by myself and this gang of boys . . ."

Mrs. Boyd listened, shifted the Mercedes into gear and drove away. And the police car had stopped beside the group of youths. An officer with a hard hat and a revolver at his belt leaned against the near-side wing. Money changed hands as Helena looked back.

"They were drug pushing," she said. "In broad daylight! And then this other boy came from the station and picked up my suitcase. He even grabbed hold of my arm!"

"I'm very sorry, dear."

Mrs. Boyd signaled a right turn, drove past a derelict high-rise office block toward the city center. Except for another police patrol car, an official limousine and a couple of taxis, the Mercedes was the only car in the street. At little more than walking pace they moved among buses, and delivery vans, and a cacophony of bicycles. Hands banged irreverently on the roof, made obscene signs at the windows. And there was a line half a mile long outside the post office.

8

"So what did he want?" asked Helena.

Mrs. Boyd sighed. "Money I expect, the same as the others."

"I mean what did Sir Gerald Fraser want?"

"He's planning to reopen a second colliery," said Mrs. Boyd. "Your father and I have been invited to join him and his wife at the Carlton on Saturday evening, to discuss it. It could mean your father being promoted to coal mines area manager."

"And what about me?" asked Helena.

"I'm afraid you're not included."

"I don't know why I bother to come home!"

"It's only for one evening," said Mrs. Boyd.

Lights in High Street might have looked nice after dark. Now they were out, and dull as the day, and several of the shops had finished trading, their windows boarded up. The arcade had been taken over by street vendors selling shoddy goods. It was all so depressing, thought Helena. And the decorated tree outside the castle did nothing to cheer her.

"Where are we going?" she asked.

"To the theater," said her mother. "I want to book tickets for the ballet. You'd like that, wouldn't you?" Helena shrugged indifferently. "I do hope you're not going to sulk for the next three weeks," said Mrs. Boyd.

She parked outside the civic center, and Helena waited in the car. The afternoon had darkened. Gray drizzle spotted the windshield, and the streets and buildings were all unlit. Trees were leafless, and the gardens bare. And the city seemed to menace her. Vagrants loitered outside a church that had been converted to a soup kitchen, and groups of young people drifted in gangs toward the shopping center. She wished she had never come to South Wales, wished she

9

had remained at school for the holidays, or stayed with one of her friends in Kent.

Then her mother returned and dropped the glossy programs in Helena's lap. And the lights came on at four o'clock. Suddenly the city was transformed, buildings winking and glimmering around Cardiff Bay as the Mercedes sped along the road to Penarth. They slowed at the checkpoint, but the security guard was a regular employee. He knew Mrs. Boyd and remembered Helena from her last visit. Without demanding their identity cards, he raised the barrier and waved them through. The city was behind them, and Helena relaxed and felt safe.

A steep street lined with exclusive shops led to the sea front. And theirs was not the only car. There was one parked outside the delicatessen, another by the wine bar, and another in the driveway of a residential home for the elderly. Christmas trees sparkled in the front rooms of large Victorian houses, and a woman wearing a fur coat walked along the esplanade without fear of attack.

Mrs. Boyd sighed. "I wish we didn't have to move," she said.

And Helena thought of it with dread.

It had been bad enough having to move from Kent, without being obliged to move again, live in some godforsaken Welsh valley with an unpronounceable name.

"Why can't we stay here?" she asked.

"You know why not," said her mother.

Helena knew.

The house in Kent was still unsold, and the present house was rented. And as manager of the colliery her father needed to be near his work, not traveling thirty miles a day. They had to go where the company sent him and they had no choice.

"Do we have a moving date yet?" she asked.

"Early March," said Mrs. Boyd.

Helena brooded, glanced at the programs in her lap. Her mother had booked three tickets in the dress circle for a production of *Swan Lake*. But Helena had seen it twice already and did not want to go.

"Ungrateful cow!"

The words echoed in her memory.

And she had not begun to think of what they meant.

■ ■ ■

The soup kitchens opened their doors. Beat music thumped in back-street basements, and under the orange streetlights brightening in the dusk, girls no older than Dilys offered to sell themselves for sex and drugs. Emanations of anger grew as Hugh walked homeward. A sleety rain was falling, soaking his parka and spangling Dilys's hair. And in places the streets were awash, water feeding back through the drains as the sea levels rose. He could sense, rather than see, all the sodden acres between himself and the estuary, reclaimed land being reclaimed again by the sea. The abandoned factories in the industrial park were never dry, except in summer droughts.

"Things are getting worse," said Hugh.

"Less than nine ecu between us," said Colin.

"Hardly worth hanging around for," said Flutey.

"I mean the water level," said Hugh. "A few weeks of rain and a couple of high tides and it'll be into the houses."

"It's the greenhouse effect," said Flutey.

"Some people are moving out already," said Dilys.

"Staying with relatives in the suburbs," said Colin.

"And what can you earn in the suburbs?" asked Hugh. "Apart from a few shops there's nothing there."

"Everyone's in the same boat," said Flutey.

"Except for a few," said Dilys. "That stuck-up English bitch at the station for example."

"I'm sick of it," said Hugh.

"But what else is there?" asked Flutey.

"Life's hard," said Colin. "And then you die."

"Cue the violins," said Hugh.

"It's true," said Dilys. "The mortality rate is increasing all the time. And there was typhoid in Hinton Street last summer."

"And how many die of AIDS?" asked Colin.

"Do you have to be so cheerful?" asked Hugh.

"So what else is there?" Flutey repeated.

"I don't know," said Hugh. "But there has to be something."

"Whistle when you find it," Colin said.

They parted at the corner . . . Dilys, Flutey and Colin heading for the public housing development, Hugh for the cramped terraces of houses nearer the river. A bag of second-hand tea bags Dilys had gotten from the station cafeteria, in exchange for fifty Styrofoam cups washed in the handbasin in the ladies' restroom, banged against his legs. Elder trees grew through the windows of a chapel, a few remaining leaves dark in the lamplight. A gang of young people passed him going in the opposite direction. They carried their music with them, the savage beat of a boom box shattering the silence. And their mood touched him, violent and resentful.

When you had nothing, ten ecu and a Christmas bonus were a lot to be deprived of.

He turned into Swindon Street and all was quiet. Drawn curtains at the windows of houses closed out the night, threadbare in places and letting the light show through, and the colored flickers of televisions. He remembered a sociology lesson he had had at school. Television was necessary, the teacher had said. It occupied people's minds, stopped them from thinking. Without it there could be mass revolution.

Inevitably it was on when Hugh reached home. At either end of the sofa his parents sat and watched . . . a children's cartoon made in America more than half a century ago. Neither of them spoke. And the room decayed around them . . . rotting skirting boards, mold on the walls and patches of damp.

"*Nos da,*" said Hugh.

"Ssh," said his mother.

"Okay," said Hugh.

He hung his parka on a hook in the hall, pegged the tea bags to dry on a line above the kitchen sink, placed the two ecu he had earned on the table, then returned to the sitting room, squatted by the gas fire, and held out his hands to the flames. The house smelled of grease and cabbage. And there were holes in his mother's slippers, runs in her stockings and a magenta patch on his father's trousers. An empty beer bottle lay on the floor by his feet; another, full one, was clasped in his hand. Hugh understood. It was just another way of escaping, dulling the ache of reality.

Music came at the end of the program.

"What's for dinner?" he asked.

"Fries and beefburgers," said his mother.

"I might have known," said Hugh. "If it's not minced meat and cabbage, it's fries and beefburgers. Forever and ever, amen. Why can't we have something different for a change?"

"When I was a child, my mother never did any cooking," said Mrs. Davies. "Food was bought ready prepared and meals were heated in the microwave oven. *I* have to stand in line for everything. *And* eke out the ration coupons."

"What's that got to do with it?" asked Hugh.

"She's just told you," said Mr. Davies.

Land of Hope and Glory introduced the five-o'clock news.

There were riots in Bristol.

The last car factory was closing down.

"You could follow the cooking lessons on TV," said Hugh.

"All that dried fruit and raw vegetables," said Mrs. Davies.

"Makes you shit regular, see?"

"Your father likes a proper meal."

"You don't know what you're talking about, Mam."

"Don't speak to your mother like that," said Mr. Davies. "If you don't like it here, you know what you can do!"

"One day I might," said Hugh.

His mother went to the kitchen.

"Is this all you earned?" she said.

■   ■   ■

The last car factory was closing down.

"There soon won't *be* any cars," said Helena.

"I think that's the general idea," said Mrs. Boyd. "We have to reduce pollution and energy consumption, don't we?

14

And with fuel at ten ecu a liter . . . who can afford to run one? We certainly couldn't, not without the company expense account."

"We're going to be stuck in that bloody valley, aren't we?"

"We can still come to Cardiff on the train."

"Until the coal supplies run out!"

"That won't happen yet awhile," said Mrs. Boyd. "It was why the government closed the mines in the first place . . . to preserve supplies for the future. Coal won't run out in our lifetime."

"That's what they said about oil once," said Helena. "That's what they said about all the other natural resources that are more or less used up. But everything runs out in the end, doesn't it?"

"Well, it's not our responsibility, Helena."

"Maybe not," said Helena. "But one day I might have to live with the consequences. And we'd be living with it now if Daddy didn't have a job. We'd be joining the ranks of the unemployed and managing on welfare benefits."

"So count yourself lucky," said her mother.

It was the end of the conversation.

Helena went upstairs to unpack her suitcase.

Scents of roast lamb and freshly baked pastry wafted from the kitchen, and Mrs. Price sang as she worked. She probably counted herself lucky, Helena thought sourly. It was better to be a paid domestic, with a husband who did gardening and odd jobs for low wages, than be dependent on government handouts. Mrs. Price even seemed to be proud of their situation. And the house was kept spotless, everything cleaned and polished, and matching towels laid out on Helena's bed.

The room was at the front with a view of the sea, a dark

15

expanse of water, and the lights of Weston on the opposite shore. She drew the pink velour curtains and frowned at the decor that was not to her taste . . . wallpaper with stripes, and stuffy magnolia paintwork, and a frieze of roses below the picture rail.

"Ungrateful cow!"

Unbidden the girl's voice spoke in her head.

And the scene replayed itself.

The boy had picked up her case.

"I've telephoned your mother, Miss Alice. . . ."

He had gray eyes and had been trying to help her. But no one did something for nothing, not these days. He had wanted money, the same as the others, her mother had said. And he had accosted her before, on the platform, offered to carry her case . . . illegally earning while his parents were claiming welfare benefits, no doubt. Nevertheless he had helped her, saved her from that other gang of boys. And she could at least have thanked him. She could have given him a few ecu for his trouble.

"Ungrateful cow!"

Helena chewed her lip. She did not know who he was, or where he came from, and probably she would never meet him again. But neither would she ever forget him. Nameless and forever, he would remain in her mind, along with her own shame.

2

On Saturday, the morning before Christmas Eve, Hugh came downstairs to the smell of baking. His mother was making an effort. Extra ration coupons had allowed for a jar of mincemeat and some cooking apples. In the sitting room his father was watching television, the inevitable bottle of beer clutched in his hand. Hugh set the kettle to boil, unpegged a tea bag from the line above the sink and dropped it in the pot.

"Started early, hasn't he, Mam?"

"You know how it is with him," Mrs. Davies said wearily.

"It doesn't have to be like that."

"Got no purpose, has he?"

"So why doesn't he find one?"

Mrs. Davies sighed.

"It is different when you are young, Hugh. But what's there for him?"

17

"There's always hope," said Hugh. "One day you might win the national lottery. Or the present recession might end. Or someone might find a way of using piss to drive the internal combustion engine, or dried crap as a fuel source. The factories could reopen, and Da might find another job . . . nine to five on the production line, just as it used to be. The good old days might come again."

"No they won't," said Mrs. Davies. "Gone forever, they have, and your father knows that. He gave up hoping long ago. On the scrap heap, he is, for the rest of his days."

Hugh switched on the grill and made toast.

There were other things in life apart from working for a living, he thought, other things that were important. Whistle when you find them, Colin had said. Hugh knew as well as anyone that the old values still remained. Money was the only commodity that really mattered . . . and a regular job the only alternative to a lifetime of poverty and hopelessness. Hugh was not immune to his father's predicament.

"Want a cup of tea, Da?"

"No, thanks," replied Mr. Davies.

Hugh mashed the tea bag, poured for himself and his mother, spread margarine on his toast, and went to join his father on the sofa. The gas fire hissed, and the wallpaper above it was brown from age and heat. Cobwebs danced. The ceiling was cracked, and paint peeled from the window. And his father sat there, drinking beer and watching television, hypnotized by the flicker and absorbing nothing. He would probably sit there for the rest of his life . . . except on Thursdays, when he cashed the welfare check and went to the pub.

"This room needs decorating, Da."

"I daresay it does," said Mr. Davies. "But there's no point

18

in spending money and energy on a place that will never be your own. It's the building society's job to maintain it, not mine. They took it away from me when I couldn't pay the mortgage."

"But we live in it, Da."

"What's that got to do with it?"

Hugh shrugged.

They had had this conversation before and it got nowhere.

He stared at the television. An enthusiastic presenter was discussing a government-sponsored program of alternative lifestyles. The possibilities of keeping chickens within the urban environment for instance. All that was needed was a small backyard, and a defunct refrigerator that could be converted to a coop.

"*We* could keep a few chickens," said Hugh.

"Your mother's got enough to do already," said Mr. Davies.

"I don't mind feeding them," said Hugh.

"On what?" asked Mr. Davies.

"Scraps," said Hugh.

"Chickens smell," said Mr. Davies. "And who's going to kill them?"

Hugh gave up.

Music played at the end of the program, and the credits rolled. Then came a five-minute talk by a Catholic bishop on the overpopulation problem and the need for single-child families. Gray daylight filtered through the window onto a carpet worn colorless by the years. And the tea was as weak as dishwater. Hugh stood up to go.

"Bring us another beer," said Mr. Davies.

"What did your last one die of?" asked Hugh.

"Don't get clever with me, boy!"

"I'm not," said Hugh. "But when you drop dead due to atrophy of the muscles, or sclerosis of the liver, I'm not being indicted for collusion, see?"

His father rose.

There were buttons missing from his shirt.

And his belly overhung his belt.

"You're asking for a clip around the lip!" he said.

The room seemed suddenly hot.

Then the electricity went out.

And so did Hugh.

■　■　■

Mr. Boyd had driven the car to work, so Helena and her mother had an early lunch and caught the train to Cardiff for some last-minute Christmas shopping.

There had been riots in several cities the last two evenings, civil unrest in many more, although according to the local radio station Cardiff remained quiet. But there was definitely an atmosphere, Mrs. Price had warned them. And security at the Central Station had been stepped up. More than a dozen guards in gray uniforms patrolled the platforms and underpasses, and there were no young people begging, no prostitutes in the entry, no sign of the boy. Unaccosted, Helena followed her mother outside.

A cold rain blew in her face, and police in riot gear patrolled the bus depot. Several more lingered on the opposite corner, gray light shining on their shields and visors, revolvers and truncheons. And there were others in St. Mary Street, white helmets moving amid a crowd of plastic rain-hoods and spread umbrellas. Multicolored Christmas lights shone brightly and the shops were all lit up, the electricity supply restored until after the festive season. Helena could feel the air of excitement, as if the undercurrents of ugliness had been driven away.

"Looks as though everything's nicely under control," said Mrs. Boyd.

"At least there are no gangs about," said Helena.

"It's good preventive policing," said Mrs. Boyd.

The traffic of buses and bicycles left ghostly tracks on the wet pavement as they crossed to the department store. Elves and reindeer pranced in the windows, and private security guards stood by the door. They smiled and apologized, searched Mrs. Boyd's handbag and demanded Helena's identity card, then let them pass through.

Inside was warm and softly lit. Christmas music played in the background, and a voice over the P.A. system announced seasonal bargains on various floors. Baubles and tinsel and metallic trees hung with parcels made a riot of color. Here, where the well-to-do of the area came to shop, there was no shortage of consumer items. Customers in smart clothes milled around the display counters . . . and Helena needed to choose presents for her father, Mrs. Boyd a present for herself—a new dress to wear at the Carlton that evening when dining with Sir Gerald Fraser.

She glanced at her wristwatch.

"I'll have a quick look upstairs, then I'll try a couple of more select boutiques," she told Helena. "So I'll meet you back here in the coffee shop at half past three. We'll have cake and coffee, and catch the four-thirty train home."

Released from her mother's company, Helena wandered around the ground floor, bought a chiffon scarf and a pair of earrings, then rode the escalator up to the men's department. It was almost empty . . . just a woman buying shirts, a fat man trying on a sports jacket, and a couple of youths half hidden by a selection of parkas. Helena examined ties, and handkerchiefs, and driving gloves, and failed to make up her mind. Maybe she would buy a tie pin? she thought. She headed toward the escalator going down.

Then a movement caught her eye. Through a rear doorway marked emergency exit she saw another two youths arrive. Their hair was long and unkempt, their clothes dirty, their movements furtive. They watched until the coast was clear, then scuttled to join the two among the parkas.

Suddenly Helena felt nervous.

But she was not the only one who had noticed.

A salesclerk approached them.

"If you gentlemen are not intending to buy . . ."

The youths turned on him.

"Who says we're not?"

"You, is it? And who are you?"

"Own the place, do you?"

Their voices, harsh and aggressive, seemed to threaten.

People turned their heads.

And Helena's fear increased.

Half a dozen other youths were coming upward on the escalator, and rather than pass them, she took to the stairs. Nothing alarming in the ladies' fashion area . . . just a group of teenage girls trying on hats . . . and no sign of her mother. She had left already, Helena supposed, and continued down the stairs.

She paused in sight of the ground floor. They were there too . . . groups of girls, groups of youths, gathering together in pools of shadows, and others mingling openly with the shoppers. She watched in alarm as a man, wearing rubber-soled shoes and a torn raincoat, approached the perfume counter. He was carrying a battered holdall that might contain weapons. People looked at him suspiciously and the security guards homed in on him. A male-voice choir sang Christmas carols over the P.A. system.

Helena hardly knew what happened next, but suddenly a woman screamed, the shoppers scattered, and the windows broke in a huge smash of sound. The young converged, and more came pouring in from the street, men, women and even children among them . . . a heaving mass of people. They were all wet, most of them filthy, all of them poorly clad . . . a lawless mob, laughing, screaming, shouting, thieving, looting, attacking. Hands reached toward the counters, grabbed whatever they found, tore down the bright decorations, smashed the lights. Missiles flew and some wielded cudgels. A girl snatched a fur hat from a woman's head. And somewhere a police whistle blew, a siren wailed.

Terrified, Helena turned to run. But they were above her too. Youths and girls came down the stairs toward her. One had a Walkman plugged into his ears. His eyes were glazed. And the expressions on all their faces were ruthless and uncaring.

"Hello, darling."

"Who's a pretty little rich girl then?"

"There's a nice scarlet coat you're wearing."

"My Mam could do with a coat like that."

"And a nice pair of boots to go with it."

"Such pretty earrings, too."

"And what's in your handbag, sweetheart?"

"Let's have a look, shall we?"

"Leave me alone!" Helena said fearfully.

■　■　■

There had been no point going to the city center that morning. A high police presence and increased security at the railway station made any chance of earning a few ecu impossible. Instead, Hugh and Dilys, Colin and Flutey targeted one of the better-class housing areas. People were not rich there, but they were employed, and there were no security checkpoints barring access . . . just a few burglar alarms, a few neighborhood-watch stickers and organized vigilante patrols in case of trouble. Hugh, Flutey, and Colin knocked on doors, asked for odd jobs, and gained nothing, although Dilys was offered a regular cleaning position with a Mrs. Wynne-Jones one morning a week.

"Any other suggestions?" asked Hugh.

"Dumpster combing?" said Flutey. "Round the back of High Street shops?"

The riot was already happening when they arrived. Windows were broken. Teenagers and children threw stones and bricks at the police. Broken strings of Christmas lights spat blue electric sparks. Bicycles lay abandoned on the sidewalks. Somebody bled from a cut on the head. A city bus burned and people rampaged through the shops, brought out all they could carry—clothes on hangers, stereo equipment, beds and sofas, washing machines. Smoke billowed from the upper floor of the main department store. Noise and madness were everywhere around them, a raging mass of humanity wherever they looked.

Voices screamed.

"Take away our Christmas bonus, would they?"

"Dock ten ecu from our benefit!"

"Well, up them!"

"Happy Christmas anyway!"

"Help yourselves, everyone!"

"Grab what you can!"

"Make the most of the opportunity!"

"Everything's free!"

"You may never get another chance like this!"

"The bastards can't jail all of us!"

"Come on!" yelled Dilys.

Hugh forced his way along the wall and in through the broken window of the department store. On the ground floor there was nothing left. The counters had been stripped of their goods, and the shoppers stripped of all they possessed . . . money and credit cards, jewelry and wristwatches, even their shoes and clothes. Half-naked women and children stood and wept, or watched in bewilderment. Bruised and beaten men lay on the floor, and the red plush carpet was gone. Smoke drifted down the stairway.

"Looks like we missed the boat," said Colin.

"We could try the basement," said Flutey.

"Or go somewhere else," said Dilys.

Hugh went up.

BRIDALWEAR, LADIES' FASHIONS, AND CORSETRY said the sign at the top of the stairs. And again the whole floor was empty, empty of people, empty of everything. The lights had been smashed, shelves and the cashier's counter broken up for wood and carried away, the cash registers looted. Gloomy daylight filtered through a window. Two men, carrying a double bed between them, came down the stairs as Hugh went on up.

"Nothing left up there, boyo," one of them said.

But Hugh went anyway . . . up through the men's department to the toy and furniture departments. A deep fryer was ablaze in the adjoining coffee shop, flames licking the walls, creeping across the floor. And Santa's grotto was on fire. The ferocity scared him. Sounds of street fighting faded in the roar of fire, and the heat drove him backward. Smoke stung his eyes and made him cough. He retreated down the stairs. And somewhere, in the ladies' fashion department, he heard someone crying.

He shouted.

And the crying stopped.

He listened and waited.

And then it began again.

"Where are you?" asked Hugh.

He found the girl in the fitting rooms. A full-length mirror reflected her huddled against the wall, stripped almost naked, nothing left to her but her bra and panties and a pair of run pantyhose. Her pale disheveled hair hung loose around her shoulders. He saw blood on her front from a cut lip, bruises on her arms, and her blue eyes gazed at him in terror. Vaguely, just for a moment, Hugh thought he recognized her, but he could not think how.

"You hurt bad, are you?"

"Leave me alone!" she whimpered. "Please, leave me alone. I haven't got any money. They've taken everything I had. And I didn't mean to sound ungrateful the other day, but I didn't know you were trying to help me. I never realized until afterward."

Hugh stared at her.

And the memory returned . . . a scarlet coat, a case on wheels.

"Is that you, Miss Helena?"

26

"Leave me alone . . . please!"

"I'm not going to hurt you, miss. But you can't stay here. There's a fire upstairs in the coffee shop and it's likely to spread. You come with me and I'll take you home."

Fresh tears welled in her eyes.

"How?" she wept. "They've taken my clothes and I don't have any shoes. And I'm supposed to be meeting my mother in the coffee shop at half past three."

"By half past three the whole place will be burned out," said Hugh. "We got to get out of here now, see?"

She was shaking violently from cold or reaction, half hysterical about all she had lost . . . her handbag, her identity and credit cards, a pair of gold earrings, a watch given to her for her birthday, and her mother. Hugh took off his parka and draped it around her shoulders, helped her find the sleeves and zip the zipper, but there was nothing he could say. Then he took off his sneakers—wet, filthy, several sizes too big, and worn to holes. He forced Helena's slim feet inside them and tied the laces.

"Let's get going, girlie," said Hugh.

She stood awkwardly.

Her legs and thighs were still exposed.

But the parka covered the worst of her nakedness.

"I can't go out looking like this!" she wailed.

"How do you mean?" said Hugh.

"What if someone sees me?"

"I'm not quite with you, Miss Helena."

"I must look absolutely awful!"

"Listen," said Hugh. "There's a riot going on! No one gives a shit what anyone looks like. You want to be thankful you're still alive!"

Helena stared at him.

He saw the anguish in her eyes fade to common sense.

"I don't even know your name," she said.

"Hugh," said Hugh. "Now are you coming with me or aren't you?"

■ ■ ■

Clutching his hand, shuffling in his shoes, Helena followed Hugh through a fire door and down the stairs. They emerged into rain and a delivery yard. Metal gates, which were usually padlocked shut, had been broken open, allowing access to a lane that led to the street. Raw cold hurt her lip, chilled her thighs, and smoke hung in a pall over the shopping center behind them. There were fights around the castle, riot police approaching from all directions, fire engines and ambulances arriving, uniformed men carrying stretchers and uncoiling hoses.

Hugh hesitated, unsure of which way to go, and Helena tugged at the parka to try and cover herself. But no one noticed either of them. And Helena might have been invisible, or nonexistent, as unkempt and impoverished as Hugh.

"Where is it you are wanting to get to?" he asked her.

"Penarth," she said.

"We'll head for the station then."

"How will I pay for a ticket?" asked Helena. "I've got no money."

"Join the club," said Hugh.

The rain turned to sleet and Helena shivered. And Hugh had bare feet and nothing but a shirt to protect him.

"What shall we do?" she asked wretchedly.

"Walk?" said Hugh.

"But it's more than five miles!" said Helena.

"You want to hang around here, do you?"

But there were roadblocks everywhere, the riot being contained, no traffic moving, and no one allowed through.

"We'll have to go to my place then," said Hugh.

Unprotesting, Helena went with him. The soaked shoes rubbed a blister on her heel, and rain dripped from her hair. They went past the prison and over the railway line, through desolate streets, past derelict shops and mean terraced houses. Trees grew through the windows of a chapel. Hard-faced women waited in doorways, and young children passed them, running homeward with their arms full of loot. Ahead of them two men carried a double bed. And side roads led off into vast treeless developments.

It was as if Helena had entered another world, an alien world that was all cold and gray and comfortless, a world that Hugh knew and she did not. The ugliness was an assault on her senses. And her bruises ached, her cut lip bled, her feet and legs froze and grew numb. The clutch of Hugh's hand was her only warmth, and she had no choice but to trust him.

Then, finally, he led her indoors, into a small, dark interior where a gas fire hissed and a television flickered. A woman, whose face she could not see, towel-dried her hair and dressed her in dry clothes. Probably she cried, although she did not remember . . . only the taste of hot sweet tea, stinging pain in her hands and feet, and lilting Welsh voices talking around her.

"Poor little *cariad*."

"Where did you say she is coming from?"

"Penarth, is it?"

"Her people are having plenty of money then?"

"And is it only her clothes they have taken?"

"Not touched her in other ways, have they?"

29

"There, there, my lovey. Never you mind."

"You'll be all right here awhile."

"We'll look after you."

The afternoon grew darker. Someone switched on the light. After a while Helena sniffed and wiped her eyes, became aware of where she was and what she was wearing. She was dressed in someone else's clothes—a brown checked skirt, an old blue sweater frayed at the cuffs, and slippers worn to holes. There was no sign of Hugh . . . just a gross-looking man sitting in a battered armchair watching television and drinking beer, and a skinny woman perched on the arm of the sofa regarding Helena with gray anxious eyes.

"Feeling better, *cariad*?"

"If I could use your telephone . . ." Helena began.

"We haven't got a telephone, my lovey."

"This is Splott, not Penarth," said the man.

"Be quiet, Mervyn!"

"She ought to know how it is to be unemployed! We got no money for fancy consumer apparatus!"

"Not her fault, is it?" said the woman.

"Not ours either!" the man said bitterly.

Helena chewed her sore lip.

She hated these people, hated this house, and she wanted to go home. But her telephone card had been stolen, along with her handbag, so there was no point in finding a public phone booth. And she had no way of paying for a taxi. For the first time in her life she knew what it meant to have no money. She was powerless, helpless, dependent on the charity of others, and forced to beg.

"If you could lend me fifty ecu . . ."

"See?" said the man. "She's got no bloody idea!"

"I'll give it you back with interest," said Helena.

"You don't understand," said the woman.

"We haven't got fifty ecu," said the man.

Helena began to feel desperate.

"So how am I going to get home?"

"Hugh has gone to see Taffy the Scrap," said the woman. "He's got a car, see? Maybe he'll take you home."

"But it'll cost you," said the man.

"I don't care how much it costs," Helena said desperately.

The man shrugged, swilled beer from a bottle.

And the woman's pores were gray with dirt.

And the house had a smell to it.

She would pay anything, anything to get out of there.

3

Christmas was over, gas and electricity restored to normal. Frost made patterns on the windows overnight and the taps in the bathroom froze. Hugh slept late, had to wash in the kitchen sink, make do with bread and jam for breakfast and tea from the thermos flask. And the television was off. His father, wearing mittens and a flea-market jacket, was reading a newspaper, and his mother sat and knitted, a blanket wrapped around her legs. Hugh perched on the arm of the sofa. A slant of sun filtered through the window, showed traces of colors that had once patterned the carpet.

"Lovely morning," said Hugh.

No one answered him.

"Yes," said Hugh. "A lovely morning. Lifts the spirits, it does, a bit of sunlight. Nice to see everyone up and doing, happy and smiling and full of the joys of living."

"That was my best skirt!" said Mrs. Davies.

"Still carrying on about it, are we?"

"At least she could have returned it!"

"Her kind doesn't know what it is to want," said Mr. Davies.

"And that was a good sweater," said Mrs. Davies. "Plenty of wear left in it. Not to mention my slippers. No way to show gratitude, is it?"

"She doesn't know what it means to be grateful," said Mr. Davies. "Couldn't wait to get out of here, could she?"

Hugh went to swill his plate under the cold tap and set it to drain. He could understand his parents' bitterness. Their values were different from Helena's. What were clothes to his mother would be rags to her. One glimpse inside her home had taught him that.

Briefly he remembered the bright light shining in a luxury kitchen, smells of roast meat, and a feeling of richness as he stood outside the door. "Wait there," Helena had said. A woman in an apron had appeared a few minutes later, given him a fifty-ecu note to give to Taffy, and closed the door. And that was the end of the incident. In a moment of sadness Hugh had accepted it. But his parents could not. Helena owed them something.

"That was my best skirt!" Mrs. Davies repeated.

"For crying out loud!" said Hugh.

"And she never even said thank you!"

"Under the circumstances is that so surprising?"

"Beneath her, was it?"

"She was caught in a riot, Mam!"

"What's that got to do with it? Her kind are all the same. Just because they have money, they think they're better than us!"

"A snob!" said Mr. Davies. "That's what she was. You want to get over there, boy, and ask for your mother's things back."

"I never asked you to lend her the blasted skirt!"

"She was wet and cold and three parts naked," said Mrs. Davies. "What else was I to do?"

"You could have chucked her out, Mam."

"Don't be stupid, Hugh."

"So don't keep on about it then!"

"Right!" said his father. "You go and get them things back and we'll have no more argument, see?"

Hugh sighed and gave in, put on his parka and the new pair of sneakers he had been given for Christmas, bought cheap from a market stand. Sometimes he wondered how much longer he could go on living in his parents' house. It was as if they were entrenched, their minds stuck in a groove, a meanness of spirit that had nothing to do with lack of money.

Over and over, all though his life, Hugh had listened as they aired their grievances, hankering backward to a different era, to the times before he was born. He tried to imagine them young and full of hope, conceiving a future for themselves . . . his father working in a factory and buying this house . . . his mother with a washing machine that actually functioned and the kitchen, like Helena's, newly fitted and full of fancy gadgets. But things broke down, unemployment reduced them, and the years eroded their dreams. Now they were old and bitter, with nothing to live for . . . and neither of them much past forty. And he, if he stayed, would be gripped by the same contagious despair.

"I'll see you later," said Hugh.

And he set out to walk to Penarth.

There was ice on the streets in places, frost on the sidewalks, and walking in the shadows Hugh could see his own breath. Soon, in the unheated houses, old people would begin to die of hypothermia. It happened every year . . . life expectancy falling as the standard of living worsened. And even as he thought it, he saw the black public works van turn into the housing development, drive at funeral pace along Cowley Road, and stop where the people were gathered. Amid silence and weeping, men of the disposal unit unloaded the body bag. There were no flowers and no coffin for those who could not pay . . . just a brief recorded service and compulsory cremation.

Somberly Hugh walked on.

Life was hard, Colin had said, and then you died.

And there was evidence of death in the city center too—fire-damaged shops, ruined buildings, and the charred remains of financial institutions . . . everything burned and blackened, soaked by water and frozen overnight, thawing in the sunlight and releasing a stench of ash. Firefighters raked at the debris. A few hardened shop owners had begun the clearing-up process, and men with clipboards and hard hats stood around and assessed the damage. But Hugh doubted if the center of Cardiff would ever live again, not as he knew it. It was gone forever, like the way of life it had represented, the heart of it destroyed in a few nights of madness.

And how many people were unemployed because of it? Hugh wondered. How many had lost their livelihoods? Salesclerks, shop assistants, cleaners, and security guards, reduced to a state of poverty, as dependent on the welfare system as all the rest. And what else was there? What else could there ever be if nothing changed in the hearts of people? Street vendors, come by bus from the outlying areas, offered vegetables for sale at inflated prices. Others sold handicrafts to anyone rich enough to pay. None of them were interested in Hugh . . . except a man selling joy drops, and two police officers who ordered him to move on.

Sunlight glittered on the swamped streets by the docks, glittered on the mud flats farther out in Cardiff Bay, and reed beds were frosted white along the river Ely as he walked the road to Penarth. It was different in daylight, grand Victorian houses built on a promontory, a steep street leading upward. He saw several cars parked outside the shops, and a delivery van passed unhindered through the checkpoint. But Hugh was stopped by the security guards, forced to produce his identity card and answer questions.

No one remembered him from the other evening. No one remembered a vintage Rolls-Royce driven by Thomas Edwards, otherwise known as Taffy the Scrap. And Hugh was unable to tell them Helena's surname, just her address, and a vague description of a house overlooking the sea. He had rescued her from the riot, he said, an English girl with long fair hair. And no, she was not expecting him.

"Best return the way you've come then," one of the guards advised him. "It's private residential, see? We can only admit pass holders and bona fide visitors."

"She vouched for me last time," said Hugh.

"That's as may be . . ."

"I only want to collect Mam's things."

"And collect the family silver while you're at it!"

"It's our job to prevent any likely theft, boy."

"That's what they pay us for, see?"

"So why don't you telephone?" asked Hugh. "Check with

her first. Tell her I'm here. Surely you know who she is? She had a scarlet coat and arrived last Thursday on the train from London."

The guards looked at each other.

"English, you say?"

"With long fair hair and a scarlet coat?"

"That's Mr. Boyd's daughter, isn't it?"

"She comes here to stay during the school holidays."

"From Kent or Sussex."

"And she *did* arrive last Thursday."

"Her mother went to fetch her from the station."

"A bit of all right, too."

"Fancy your chances, do you, boy?"

"Give her a bell, shall we?"

"See what she has to say?"

The guards winked and guffawed, and outside the hut Hugh stood and waited, a lower-class citizen needing Helena's permission to proceed along what had once been a public highway. On the right foot of his new sneakers the sole had already come unstuck. And icicles thawed in the sun.

■　■　■

Holidays were boring, thought Helena, nothing to do and nowhere to go and no one to talk to. Her father had returned to work and her mother was still feeling fragile after her experiences in the riot. Not that anything in particular had happened to Mrs. Boyd. She and the manager of the boutique had escaped through a back alley and locked themselves in a public restroom until the riot police rescued them the following morning. But now she was agoraphobic, afraid to go out, and the doctor had prescribed tranquilizers to calm her nerves. Mrs. Price took her breakfast in bed, and Helena had no company but her own.

She sat in her bedroom reading a book and waiting for lunchtime. The room was cold, the heating switched off until one o'clock, although outside the sunlight glimmered on a tranquil sea, and tall ships with white sails headed along the Bristol Channel. The Somerset Hills were blue smudges on the far horizon. And downstairs in the kitchen Mrs. Price sang operatic arias.

"Do ask her to be quiet," called Mrs. Boyd.

"She's only singing," said Helena.

"So ask her to sing more quietly, please."

"Maybe she's feeling happy," said Helena. "People do sing when they're happy."

"Well, I've got a headache," said Mrs. Boyd.

"And I'm trying to read," said Helena.

"Why do you always have to argue?" said Mrs. Boyd. "It's not much to ask, is it? Just tell her to be quiet, and bring me a couple of aspirin. And take my tray down when you go."

"Bloody hell!" said Helena. "You're not that ill! What I went through was far worse than anything that happened to you! And I'm not your slave either!"

She flounced into her mother's bedroom, snatched up the tray, and went stamping downstairs to the kitchen. Soup simmered on the bottled-gas stove, and Mrs. Price was on her hands and knees, singing the overture from *Carmen* and polishing the linoleum. An old brown-checked skirt buffed it to a fine shine. And Helena remembered . . . a dingy house, a battered sofa, herself sitting before the gas fire wearing that same skirt.

She shuddered convulsively.

Unemployment was a fact of life for a large percentage of the population. But she had not known what it meant until she experienced it for herself.

She shuddered again. She had tried to forget what happened, but now it returned to her, nightmare memories being replayed . . . scenes in the department store, grabbing hands and hard faces, a fur hat snatched from a woman's head . . . the group on the stairs, their eyes, their voices, her own terror. They had taken her watch and shoulder bag, pulled out her earrings, stripped her of her clothes. She remembered someone laughing, a girl with a mouthful of rotten teeth and eczema on her hands.

She had thought it was greed that drove them, jealousy because she had more than they did. But Hugh had not been like that. His voice had been kind and he had tried to take care of her. She remembered the horrible unwashed smell of his parka, and the stinking wetness of his shoes. She remembered the vile cabbagy reek of the house he had taken her to.

He lived there, she thought.

He actually lived there.

In a state of poverty she could not have imagined a week ago.

It made her feel sick just to think of it.

And Mrs. Price was polishing the floor with his mother's skirt.

It was all it was fit for, Mrs. Boyd had said.

She had no idea, thought Helena.

Then the telephone rang.

Mrs. Price stopped singing, and Helena placed the tray on the countertop. All the unwanted thoughts fled from her head, and she returned, thankfully, to the normality of her own existence. It might be Patti telephoning from Kent, or her father to say he would be late home for dinner. Upstairs Mrs. Boyd called for someone to answer it, and Helena picked up the receiver.

"Hello?"

It was the security guard from the checkpoint. He said he had a person outside wanting to collect his mother's things.

"Pardon?" said Helena.

"A person by the name of Davies," said the guard.

"I don't know anyone . . ."

"Hugh Davies?"

"Oh yes," said Helena.

"He says you'll vouch for him, miss."

"What did you say he wanted?"

"His mother's things, miss. One pair of slippers, one blue sweater, and a brown-checked skirt. He says it's her best."

"Oh," said Helena. Her mind froze. Guilt feelings lurched in her stomach, and frantically she tried to think of an excuse. "Yes, well . . . we're about to go out . . . so it's not convenient for him to come right now. And Mrs. Price has just washed the skirt. Tell Hugh we'll have everything delivered as soon as possible . . . maybe tomorrow."

She replaced the telephone. Mrs. Price stared at her, the remains of Hugh's mother's skirt in her hand. And Mrs. Boyd came downstairs in her dressing gown.

"Who was that?" she asked.

"Hugh," said Helena.

"I don't know anyone of that name."

"He helped me escape from the riot," said Helena.

"Oh yes," said Mrs. Boyd. "So what did he want?"

"His mother's skirt," said Helena. "And the sweater and

slippers we threw in the garbage. It's her best skirt, apparently. Her *best* skirt . . . would you believe it? And he wants it back."

"Oh dear," said Mrs. Boyd. "It never occurred to me."

"I tore it up for rags," said Mrs. Price.

"So what are we going to do?" asked Helena.

"We'll have to send them the money," said Mrs. Boyd.

"I don't know his address," said Helena.

"Well, in that case there's nothing we *can* do," said Mrs. Boyd. "And I don't suppose it matters very much. The boy's not likely to cause trouble, is he? Not likely to come back. Just forget about him, dear. Put the whole incident behind you."

But Helena felt bad.

Her conscience troubled her.

And she owed things to Hugh.

■ ■ ■

It was late afternoon, the sun already setting in a sky of fire and the streets turning frosty again, when Hugh reached the housing development. A short stint on the railway station had earned him nothing and there was no point in going home. He walked down Cowley Road. Drawn curtains at the windows of several houses commemorated the one who had died that morning, and farther on an ambulance was parked.

Hugh paused.

If the public health authority had sent an ambulance, it had to be something nasty, and probably contagious. Neighbors had gathered. There were whispers of smallpox, and a child wrapped in a blanket was carried from the house. He hurried past, and the sole of his shoe flapped like a tongue

41

as he went up the crumbling concrete path that led around the back of Number Eighty-nine.

It was housing trust property that had once belonged to the city council, a run-down semidetached, built midway through the last century. There was a smell of drains, and the door had fallen from the outhouse, and a broken upstairs window was mended with adhesive tape. Laundry stiffened on the garden line. But things were beginning to look up since Mrs. Williams had met her latest man. A pile of coke lay among tussocks of grass that had once been a lawn, and the back door had been freshly painted.

Hugh entered without knocking.

The kitchen was warm. Dilys sat by the newly installed coke stove nursing a cold, and two younger children were playing on a rag mat with a set of wooden bricks, and Mrs. Williams was cooking sausages and onions. She was bold faced, ample bosomed, with the same red hair inherited by her children. A hussy, according to Hugh's mother . . . her skirts too short, her sweaters too tight . . . a woman of easy virtue. But Hugh liked her. And it was not easy bringing up a family of five with only a reduced benefit allowed for the last three.

Voices chorused.

"Hi, Hugh!"

"Hello, Hugh *bach*."

And the smell of sausages made his stomach curdle with hunger.

"You want a hot dog, Hugh?" asked Mrs. Williams.

He shook his head.

The sausages would be counted, one for each.

"Mam'll have the tea ready when I get home," said Hugh.

"Better not spoil my appetite. I only popped by to see how Dilys was."

Dilys sniffed.

"Our Jimmy's got it now," she said.

"He's up in bed," said Mrs. Williams. "Running a temperature, he is, and poorly with it."

"There was an ambulance outside Number Twenty-seven," said Hugh. "Smallpox, the neighbors said."

"Oh Christ!" said Mrs. Williams.

Dilys sniffed again.

"Maybe we ought to call in the doctor, Mam."

"Where would I get fifty ecu from for a doctor's visit?"

"You could ask Bill to lend it to you."

Mrs. Williams thought for a moment and shook her head.

"No," she said firmly. "Bill's done enough for us already. I don't want him to think I'm only interested in him because he's got a job. Jimmy's caught your cold, that's all it is. I'll go round and see Granny this evening, get him some elderberry syrup."

"Where's Colin?" asked Hugh.

"Gone with Flutey looking for firewood," said Dilys. "And why aren't you with them?"

"I had to go to Penarth," said Hugh.

Dilys sniffed again.

"Chasing after *her*, I suppose!"

"Mam wanted her skirt back," said Hugh.

"Well, that provided the excuse," said Dilys.

"It's not like that," said Hugh.

"No?" said Dilys.

"No," said Hugh.

"Been mooning about her all over Christmas, you have!

Defending her and taking her side. Poor Helena. What a dreadful thing to happen. Makes you ashamed to be Welsh, it does. Well poor Helena, my foot! She's rolling in it! And you've got nothing. She'll not look twice at you, Hugh. And you must be stupid if you think it could ever be any other way!"

In the darkening room Hugh stood silenced by her words. She was as bitter as his parents, hating for the same kind of reasons. And maybe he *had* been stupid. Maybe he had hoped that Helena would want to see him. Maybe he had even hoped they could be friends. And why not? he thought. They were both human beings, weren't they?

"So you went to Penarth," said Dilys. "Go on then . . . what happened next?"

"Nothing," said Hugh.

"What d'you mean, nothing?"

"She was going out," said Hugh. "And I never got past the checkpoint."

"Now there's a shame," said Dilys. "You walked five miles there and five miles back for nothing. And what about your Mam's skirt?"

"She's sending it round."

"More likely she's torn it up for dishrags!"

"Why should she do that?"

"Because," said Dilys, "she hasn't got a clue how the other half live and, what's more, she doesn't care. You've been had for a sucker, Hugh! So you may as well forget her!"

Coke slipped on the fire.

Mrs. Williams cut hunks of bread.

And the children sat listening.

Why, wondered Hugh, should he want to forget Helena? She was like no other girl he had ever met before, clean and

44

bright, and smelling of soap and flowers. And why should Dilys want him to forget her?

Then, suddenly, it was four o'clock. The main electric light came on and caught them staring at each other. Her hair was red, like her mother's, but her blue eyes were harder, fiercer, much more proud. And he realized she hated Helena for more personal reasons. Dilys, Colin's younger sister, was growing toward womanhood and harboring designs. His future flashed before him: a decaying house like this one . . . raising kids . . . having no job . . . living hand to mouth until they both grew old.

"Are you sure you won't have a hot dog?" asked Mrs. Williams.

"No, thank you," said Hugh.

"Go on," said Dilys. "You must be hungry."

"Jimmy won't be wanting his," said Mrs. Williams.

"I've got to go," said Hugh.

"Where?" asked Dilys.

Hugh did not know.

But soon, somehow, he had to go somewhere.

Because there had to be more than this.

There had to!

4

It was the first Friday in January. Dilys had gone cleaning for Mrs. Wynne-Jones, and Hugh, Colin, and Flutey headed for the city center. Fog shrouded the streets, sea mists creeping inland making dark ghosts of the ruined buildings, muffling the wheels of bicycles and footsteps of people passing through. No point in anyone hanging around, thought Hugh. Nothing left for the pickpockets and shoplifters in the burned-out department store . . . no customers to steal from or beg from . . . no dumpsters anymore behind High Street shops. And nothing left to entice the businessmen or bankers, insurance brokers or entrepreneurs. The inner docks had been converted into housing units long ago, and those to seaward were mostly swamped and derelict, disused wharves attracting little trade. Cardiff was dead, assistance from Brussels its only hope of resurrection. But for Hugh there was no hope, not if he stayed.

There were scant pickings at the railway station. Departing trains were crowded, but those arriving brought mainly students for the university due to begin the new term.

So what was there to stay for? asked Hugh.

And what could they hope for?

Nothing, except a continuation of what was.

Or a gradual worsening.

"See what I'm getting at, do you?"

"You reckon we ought to go," said Colin.

"Where?" asked Flutey.

"And are things any better anywhere else?" asked Colin. "I mean, it's a world recession, isn't it? It'll be the same everywhere, surely?"

"But it's worse in the cities," said Hugh. "There's more of us. And there's no available land, so we can't grow our own food . . . and no trees for fuel. We've got no other way to survive. We're scavengers, for God's sake! And that may be better than being pimps, or pushers, or fixers, but as a way of life it's pretty bloody hopeless! If we go somewhere else we might have a chance of finding some kind of alternative existence."

"I dunno," Colin said dubiously.

They sat on a bench at the Central Station. Dim shapes of security men guarded a tram full of mail at the far end of the platform and failed to notice them, and on another platform the train from Penarth discharged its passengers. Fog and steam and smoke smelling of rotten eggs drifted and shifted and deprived everything of color. People gathering for the train to Paddington were gray shapes without distinction. And baggage handlers were superfluous, although Flutey offered.

"Carry your bags, sir?"

47

"Carry your bags, madam?"

"No thank you!" a woman said curtly.

She was an Englishwoman emerging from the underpass, wearing a bright cerise coat and matching hat, accompanied by a girl in a navy blue duffle coat. Just for a moment Hugh watched them. The girl had a suitcase with wheels, which she towed behind her. But it had no stickers, and her face was hidden by her hood. And maybe it was the woman who reminded him of Helena.

"What have you got to stay for?" asked Hugh. "If your Mam invites Bill to live with her, she won't be wanting you around, will she?"

"She won't do that," said Colin. "It's cohabiting and she'd lose her allowance."

"So it'll be one less mouth to feed," said Hugh.

"What about Dilys?" asked Colin.

"She can come, too, if she wants," said Hugh.

Colin frowned.

"I dunno," he repeated. "If I knew what we were going to, it might be different. But the minute we leave home, we'll be classed as vagrants, won't we? If we're vagrants, we won't qualify for welfare . . . and we don't qualify anyway because we're underage. And if we can't find a job, then how will we live? At least if we stay here, our parents can go on claiming for us. We've got a roof over our heads and meals provided. And when we're nineteen we'll have ninety ecu a week and be able to pay our way."

"And when we're twenty-five," said Hugh, "we'll have one hundred ecu a week . . . and a hundred and ten ecu a week if we live to be seventy. Now there's ambition for you! Come on, Colin! There's got to be more than this! There's got to!"

48

Flutey returned to the bench.

"That was a waste of time," he said.

"And a waste of our lives if we go on as we are," said Hugh.

"We could go and work for Taffy the Scrap," said Colin. Hugh considered it.

Working for Taffy was seldom legal. Mostly he dealt in the black market: substandard clothes imported from God alone knew where, and reconditioned household goods passed off as new . . . contraband liquor either stolen or smuggled, and ditto the cigarettes and drugs. And no one got rich working for Taffy, except Taffy himself. He might dress in scruffy clothes, live in the same kind of mean terraced house that Hugh lived in . . . but everyone knew of the Rolls-Royce kept in a lock-up garage, and the top floor of a warehouse loaded with merchandise, and where to go to for an unofficial loan to fend off the tax collectors. If they worked for Taffy, thought Hugh, they might end up as debt collectors demanding money with menaces, or peddling joy drops.

"I dunno," said Hugh.

"It might be worth a try," said Flutey.

"We've got nothing to lose," said Colin.

But they had, thought Hugh.

They could lose their self-respect . . . cheat their friends, intimidate their families, worsen the lot of their own kind. The thought disturbed him . . . like selling his soul to the Devil. And over the public address system a tinny voice announced the next train arriving . . . the ten seventeen to London Paddington, stopping at Newport, Bristol Parkway, Swindon and Reading.

"Cardiff! This is Cardiff! Change here for stations to Barry Island, Rhymney . . ."

Black, gleaming, with a squeal of brakes, amid clouds of smoke and thundrous noise, the engine ground to a halt. Carriage doors opened. One or two passengers alighted, and others boarded. The girl in the navy blue duffle coat heaved in her suitcase, and the woman in the cerise coat and hat lingered on the platform, waiting to see her depart. A face appeared at the window of a carriage, clean, bright, framed by drifts of long fair hair. Briefly, for one split second, Helena glanced at Hugh. But then, quite deliberately, she looked away, mouthed words to her mother and waved good-bye.

Something died in Hugh.

And then it no longer mattered where he went or what he did, if he stayed in Cardiff or left for somewhere else. His future was irrelevant. Any hope he might have had, and all the plans he might have made, were postponed indefinitely. He rose from his seat, turned his back on his former self and headed toward the station exit.

"Where are we going?" asked Flutey.

"*I'm* going to see Taffy the Scrap," said Hugh.

■   ■   ■

To replace the scarlet coat that had been stolen, Helena had bought a navy blue duffle coat with a hood, warm and sensible and unassuming. Hardly becoming, said Mrs. Boyd. But that was why Helena chose it. She wanted to remain anonymous, not advertise the fact that her parents had money and attract people's attention, not while she lived in South Wales. And her boots had been chosen for the same reason, dull black leather with rubber soles, flat and clumpy, and grimed with sand and salt from a walk along the seashore.

Her shoulder bag, too, was subdued navy blue, and she had removed the vacation stickers from her suitcase. Almost she felt like a different person.

"You look really drab," said Mrs. Boyd. "Why on earth didn't you put on a nice colorful scarf, cheer yourself up a bit?"

"I didn't think about it," said Helena.

"And you could at least have cleaned your boots!" said Mrs. Boyd. "Or asked Mrs. Price to do it for you. Polish isn't that expensive, you know."

The train from Penarth stopped at Cardiff Central.

Helena pulled up her hood to hide her face.

"It's not *that* cold," said Mrs. Boyd.

"The fog makes my hair go lank," said Helena.

Mrs. Boyd sniffed. "No one's likely to notice you anyway looking like that."

That was the idea, thought Helena. Yet her heart hammered with irrational fear as she walked along the platform. And, emerging from the underpass, she saw him immediately, sitting on one of the station benches next to a boy with red hair. Hugh had not changed. His eyes were gray, just as she remembered them, and he wore the same shabby parka, the same stinking shoes. She kept her face averted, trailed in her mother's wake as they approached. Another boy, a small scruffy black boy with buck teeth, offered to carry her case.

"No thank you!" her mother said curtly.

He tried someone else and eventually gave up, joined Hugh and the other boy on the bench. Helena observed them, deep in conversation, as she waited for the London train. She watched the fleeting expressions on Hugh's face, noticed the gestures of his hands and the way his hair curled around his collar. He was a mixture of strength and gentleness, she thought, and there was an openness about him that she had never come across before. And why was she so afraid of him? Why didn't she just go and say hello, thank him for all he had done for her, and apologize about his mother's skirt?

She had no time to wonder. The train arrived, in a gale of wind and noise. Smoke and soot blew in her face as the locomotive passed her. Lighted carriages slowed and stopped.

"Cardiff! This is Cardiff!"

"Do you have your ticket?" asked Mrs. Boyd.

"Yes," said Helena.

"And your new identity card?"

"Yes," said Helena.

"Don't forget to telephone me when you get there."

"I won't," said Helena.

A man opened the carriage door and she hauled the heavy suitcase inside. She left it in the luggage space, pulled off her hood, and headed down the aisle toward a vacant window seat. Then she looked out . . . and there was Hugh looking at her. Feelings shot through her . . . guilt, and shame, and everything she was. She had to look away because she could not bear it.

Her mother waved.

"See you at Easter," Helena mouthed.

And that was the last she saw of Hugh. Even before the train departed, he rose from his seat and turned his back on her, was gone through the station exit without a second glance. It seemed a deliberate act of rejection and she chewed her lip to hold back her tears. Forget about him, her mother

had said. But she could not forget. Hugh had revealed her
to herself.

■   ■   ■

It was all Taffy offered them: work on a landfill site beside
the river, marsh reverting to marsh as the sea levels rose.
Mountains of garbage, buried in the last century, were
slowly being uncovered, eroded away by human hands. Old
and young alike spent their days combing through the debris
of black plastic bags for anything that might be of value.
Aluminum cans or copper piping, strips of lead from old
windows, bits of iron or brass . . . whatever might be re-
smeltable or reusable Taffy would buy. Cash at the end of
each afternoon, he had said. And a handcart stood nearby
waiting to be filled.

It was a disgusting job. Water seeped upward through the
ground, soaked through their shoes, and their hands were
clogged with mud. Fog drifted like smoke from the estuary,
damp and chilling, isolating them even from each other.
Their fingers froze, and with everything they touched they
disturbed a stench of rottenness and decay. Hugh pulled
away shreds of material attached to the frame of an old lamp-
shade.

"Whose idea was this?" he asked.

"At least we know we'll get paid for it," said Colin.

"And Taffy might offer us something better later on,"
said Flutey.

Springs from a mattress clattered on the handcart.

And Colin unearthed another bag.

Plastic cracked and split as he pulled it free, releasing its
contents and odors—bones of animals and remnants of skin
and hair.

"Phew!" said Hugh. "A good thing Dilys didn't come. At five ecu for a morning's cleaning, she's got it made."

"Someone was watching the house," said Colin.

"You mean your house?" asked Flutey.

"No," said Colin. "Mrs. Wynne-Jones' house . . . where Dilys goes cleaning. A snooper, she said, on the other side of the street."

It was a way of making money for some people . . . informing to the welfare department on someone who was cohabiting or working illegally. They were paid a bounty of one hundred ecu for each successful prosecution.

"Dilys is in the clear anyway," said Hugh.

"She's not nineteen," said Flutey.

"Not signing on in her own right," said Hugh.

"But she's supposed to declare it," said Colin. "It's casual wages, isn't it? If the welfare find out, they'll dock it off Mam's allowance. You know the rules."

Hugh dragged out the rusting wheel of a bicycle.

He knew.

Private enterprise was not to be encouraged. If you were registered as unemployed, you were not allowed to earn anything without declaring it. And if you were caught working for money while receiving benefits, then you were hauled in front of a judge and ordered to pay it back. And if you declared what you were earning, then you had it deducted from your welfare check. So you could never win, not legally, not if you were unemployed.

The only hope was to get a real job, thought Hugh. Except there weren't any. Vacancies got filled by word of mouth, and he had left school knowing he would be unemployed forever. Forever . . . caught in the poverty trap . . . working on a garbage dump for Taffy the Scrap, and hoping

54

the welfare did not find him. Forever . . . with his life going nowhere . . . and all he might have been bartered away for the rudiments of survival. And Helena with her fair hair, and her mouth full of peaches and cream, not knowing what it was to be born poor.

"You got something on your mind?" asked Colin.

"No more than usual," said Hugh.

■ ■ ■

The fog thickened, and the afternoon grew colder, darker. People moved as shapes in the mist, and metal clattered in half a dozen handcarts heading for Taffy's scrap yard. Human voices faded in the distance, and an eerie silence gathered as Hugh, Flutey, and Colin worked on. Their breath smoked. Hoarfrost whitened around them, and Flutey's hair grew pale with rime.

Soon it was too dark to see.

Hugh blew on his hands.

"Call it a day, shall we?"

The handcart was heavy. Its wheels sank into frozen puddles and jammed against stones as they maneuvered it across the dump. Then it was easier. A broken gate gave access to a half mile of road that led between swamped factories and jungles of buddleia trees. Past winters had heaved up the asphalt, and the fog above the distant city glowed a baleful orange.

A yellow halo surrounded the light in Taffy's scrap yard.

High wooden gates rattled shut behind them.

"I've been waiting for you," said Taffy. "Over half an hour, see? Stop for a picnic by the river, did you?"

He was a thin weasely man with sandy hair and piercing blue eyes. His clothes were tattered—a sports jacket with torn pockets and trousers tied around the waist with string. But his Wellington boots were new, and he wore a fob watch on a chain. And two burly bodyguards leaned against the hood of a battered van.

"We were hoping to fill the cart," said Hugh.

Taffy glanced at the contents.

"Not too bad for half a day," he said.

"So how much will you give us?" asked Hugh.

Taffy felt in his trouser pocket and pulled out a gold cigarette case, opened it carefully and displayed the contents . . . hundreds of tiny white tablets small as saccharines.

"Know what these are?"

"Joy drops?" said Hugh.

"Work for me regular and I can supply you, see?"

"No, thank you," said Hugh.

"We know what they do," said Colin.

"People get hooked," said Flutey.

"You promised us cash, Mr. Edwards," said Hugh.

"Ah well." Taffy pocketed the cigarette case and pulled out a wad of notes. "How about five ecu?" he said.

"For three of us? For a whole afternoon's work?"

"Six then?"

"Ten," said Hugh.

"Seven," said Taffy.

"We could take it elsewhere."

"Not in my handcart," said Taffy. "And not if you want to go on working for me, either."

"Whose side are you on?" asked Hugh.

Taffy grinned.

"Only one side in this war, boy, and that's your own. Every man for himself, it is. And seven ecu is being generous, see? So do you want it or don't you?"

They accepted, because they had no choice.

And Taffy closed the gates behind them.

"We've been exploited," Colin said dully.

"And will we go on being exploited?" asked Hugh.

"What else is there?" said Flutey.

Hugh clenched his fists.

A train whistle sounded from far away. Hugh remembered Helena's face through the window, blue eyes that had looked at him and looked away. He felt betrayed: betrayed by Helena, betrayed by Taffy, betrayed by everyone . . . leaving him nothing but the anger inside him.

■　■　■

Helena could no longer see the outlines of the Kent countryside. It was dark beyond the window, and a lighted carriage crowded with commuters returning from London was reflected in the glass, along with her own face. Silently, she rehearsed once more the story she would tell her friends at school.

There had been a riot in Cardiff, and she had been caught up in it. Clear in her mind was an image of herself cowering half naked in the women's changing rooms, terror that would haunt her for the rest of her life . . . and an image of Hugh who had come to her rescue, tall and lean, and strong and gentle, his eyes gray as seawater, gray as the weather . . . their escape through the back streets of the city, the pouring rain and his hand holding hers. All that was indelible, unalterable, etched in her brain.

But the truth ended there.

What followed was altered: the house he had taken her to, small and neat, scented with lavender and clean as a new pin . . . and his parents, poor as they were, feeding her, clothing her, caring for her as if she were their own daughter. Hugh had found someone with a car to take her home. Then, later, after Christmas, he had come to inquire how she was. They had walked along the shore and fallen in love. But her mother forbade her to see him again, because he was unemployed and had no prospects . . . although they met, briefly, at the railway station, to say good-bye.

It was so sad Helena almost cried. And most of it was lies . . . facts embroidered by her imagination, turning into a fantasy that had never happened. But it might have, she thought, if she had behaved differently. She should have gone to him at the station and given him the money to replace his mother's skirt, tried to help him, as he had helped her.

Streetlights outside made the darkness orange.

And the intercom crackled above her head.

"Ladies and gentlemen, the train is approaching Ashford. Ashford is the next station stop."

People rose from their seats.

Helena buttoned her duffle coat, pulled up her hood.

There was bound to be something she could do for Hugh, something she could give that would put things right between them. A new parka, perhaps, or a new pair of sneakers? Clothes for his mother, or a food hamper? Or a job perhaps? Employment in the colliery? A career with the British Mining Company? Yes, thought Helena. That was it! That was what she would do!

There was an excitement inside her, an absurd joy that atoned for all she had felt and been ashamed of, and everything she had failed to say or do. Tonight she would telephone Penarth and ask to speak to her father. Hugh did not know it yet, but Helena was going to change his life.

5

Through the dark winter months Hugh became part of Helena's life. In the dormitory of the private school she talked of him, and in between lessons she thought of him, mapped out his future alongside her own. The British Mining Company would see his potential, train him for a position in management similar to her father's. And she herself would have a parallel career, a well-paid post in a financial institution. And in her mind Hugh was glad for her, as she would be glad for him.

Spring came early. Her parents moved to the renovated farmhouse in Ynysceiber. And in Kent the apple orchards were pink and blooming, trees and hedges tinged with new green, and gardens bright with flowers.

In April Helena packed her suitcase, put on her drab navy blue duffle coat and returned to South Wales. She was gripped by a feeling of excitement, a mixture of joy and anticipation. But clouds gathered the farther west she traveled, and her journey became a slow transition back to winter, to bare boughs and blackthorn flowers, fields of bitten grass and the occasional daffodil. The wind was chill, and the sky overcast, when she left the train at the Cardiff Station.

A crowd of young people swarmed around her, Welsh voices begging for money, offering to find her a taxi or carry her case. But Hugh was not among them, nor could she see him along the length of the platform. She followed the rest of the passengers down the steps and through the underpass to the station lobby. Drafts whistled through the broken doors. A vagrant searched the litter bins. A group of girls accosted a man with a briefcase, and begging children were everywhere. But again Hugh was not among them.

Dragging her case, Helena went to search the other platforms . . . the restrooms and waiting rooms, snack bar and cafeteria. A group of youths by the book stand nudged each other and snickered, and she remembered what had happened the last time she had arrived there. Her disappointment changed to anxiety. The station grew threatening. She had lied to her mother, told her the train arrived half an hour later than it did to give herself time . . . time to talk to Hugh, to buy him a meal in the cafeteria, perhaps, and tell him the news. It had not occurred to her he might not be there.

She returned to the foyer, waited aimlessly. The vagrant approached her, asking for money, and everyone watched her to see what she would do.

"Go away!" she said coldly.

The security guards echoed her command.

Three of them came through the underpass.

And the lobby emptied.

"Are you waiting for someone, miss?"

"My mother," said Helena.

They tipped their caps. "Better wait in the cafeteria," they advised her.

At least it was warm in the cafeteria. Red vinyl seats offered a kind of comfort, and no one was there apart from herself and the woman serving behind the counter. Helena ordered a sweet bun and a cup of coffee, sat at a table by the window, and stared gloomily out. Probably she would never see Hugh again. And if he ever thought of her, he would think of her badly, or forget she ever existed.

"If you don't want that bun, miss . . . ?"

Helena had not noticed when the girl came to join her. But she noticed her now . . . thin faced and scrawny, with huge hungry eyes, maybe ten or eleven years old, and too young to be threatening. She wore a dirty brown parka with a broken zipper, and several sizes too small.

Helena pushed the plate toward her.

"You can have it," she said.

"Gosh," said the girl.

A skinny hand reached for the bun and she ate wolfishly.

"Thank you, miss. I suppose you wouldn't consider buying another one for our William? Or a burger maybe? Da's out of work, see? And the welfare don't pay up until Thursday. And William's not been too well lately. So if you could spare a couple of ecu . . ."

Helena regarded her.

She was greed motivated, out for what she could get.

"I wonder if you could find someone for me and give him a message?" Helena asked her.

"Who?" asked the girl.

"His name's Hugh Davies," said Helena.

■ ■ ■

That winter, smallpox became epidemic in the urban housing projects. Children died, including Jimmy Williams. It was hard to believe, said Dilys, almost as if he was not dead but had gone away for a while and would one day return. But Mrs. Williams grieved and grew depressed. She had debts for doctor's bills of over five hundred ecu, and Colin worked as he had never worked before . . . all day and every day on the landfill site beside the river.

March winds dried the mud to the hardness of concrete, then the rain and spring tides softened it again. But soon, when the summer drought set in, the dump would become unworkable . . . black plastic bags preserved in shale and unretrievable without a pickaxe.

"We'll have to find another source of income," said Colin.

"Doing what?" asked Hugh.

"I don't know," said Colin. "But there has to be something."

Flutey threw an old aluminum saucepan on the handcart.

"If Hugh and I gave you one ecu a day from what we earn . . ."

"Don't be stupid!" said Colin.

"But if it'll help your Mam . . ."

"She wouldn't accept."

"She doesn't have to know," said Hugh. "And isn't that how things ought to be? Helping each other instead of helping ourselves?"

He salvaged another bag. The contents scattered, and overhead the sea gulls sailed like scraps of blown paper.

And everywhere around him he saw people abandoning their handcarts and scurrying away. Beyond the dump the forest of buddleia bushes grew green with the coming spring, and a car drove along the road between the abandoned factories, slowed and stopped at the gateway. A man got out, smartly dressed even from that distance, and headed toward them.

"Who's that?" asked Flutey.

"Welfare?" said Colin.

"We'd better leg it then."

"Why?" asked Hugh. "We're not doing anything we shouldn't be doing, are we? Just collecting bits of metal for our own purposes. If we run now, he's going to know we're guilty of something."

They waited.

Clouds scudded before the wind.

And the air smelled of rain.

"Good afternoon," the man said pleasantly. "May I see your identity cards, please."

"If we can see yours," said Hugh.

Within the European Community everyone was issued a plastic identity card stating name, birthdate, present address, and national insurance number, and a photograph of the holder on the front that was renewable every ten years. Once over the age of consent it was advisable to carry it with you at all times. And the man was not from the welfare department, but from the tax department. He was looking for a person named Thomas Edwards who was rumored to be running a scrap-metal business.

"Never heard of him," said Hugh.

"Me neither," said Colin.

"Who do the handcarts belong to?"

"I don't know about the others," said Hugh, "but this one's ours."

"You're in the scrap-metal business yourself, are you?"

"We're students," said Hugh.

"From the polytechnic," said Colin.

"The art department," said Hugh. "We make things, see?"

"Metal sculptures," said Flutey.

"For exhibitions," said Colin.

"Welsh dragons mostly," said Hugh. "We are cutting the scales out of aluminum cans and welding them together."

The man nodded.

A few spots of rain beaded his coat.

And his shiny leather shoes were smeared with mud.

"I'll believe you," he said. "Although thousands wouldn't. But perhaps I should warn you that it is illegal to sell Welsh dragons, or any other work of art, without declaring the proceeds to the tax department, or to the welfare department if you are unemployed."

"Unless it is your personal property for a period of seven years, and the net income gained is less than five hundred ecu per annum," said Hugh.

The man smiled.

"I'm glad you are aware of your rights, young man. We do our best to keep members of the public informed. And if you can't help me with the whereabouts of Thomas Edwards, I may as well try elsewhere. We shall be watching the road out of here for the next month or so, of course. Have a nice day."

They watched him picking his way through the mud toward the gateway. And ten or twelve ecus worth of scrap metal, which would never be converted into money, lay in Taffy's handcart.

"Damn!" said Hugh.

"Bang goes any hope of paying Mam's doctor's bill," sighed Colin.

"What'll we do now?" asked Flutey.

The car drove away. Then someone came running toward them, a gangly child waving her hands in the air. Above her the sea gulls screamed and wheeled, and her brown parka flapped like wings in the wind. Her voice was breathless and shrill.

"Do any of you know Hugh Davies? He lives in Splott, and I asked at the shop, and they said he'd be here. Do you know where I can find him?"

"You already have," said Hugh.

The child grinned.

"There was a girl at the station," she said. "Her name's Helena Boyd and she paid me ten ecu to deliver a message. There's work, she said, at the colliery in Ynysceiber. Three hundred and fifty ecu a week!"

Hugh and Colin looked at each other.

And their eyes shone.

■ ■ ■

"You gave her ten ecu?" said Mrs. Boyd.

"What's wrong with that?" asked Helena.

"There's one born every minute!" said Mrs. Boyd. "Really, Helena, how can you be so stupid? That child must have been laughing all the way home!"

"What else could I have done?" asked Helena.

"I don't know why you're bothering at all," said Mrs. Boyd. "You've only met the boy once."

"Twice," said Helena.

"Once . . . twice . . . what difference does it make? And

all that hassle over the telephone, persuading your father to arrange a job for him! His kind don't want to work. They're layabouts, all of them!"

Helena stared at the chocolate éclair on her plate. It was not like that, she thought, not with Hugh. And who in their right mind would actively choose to be unemployed and live in poverty? Her mother was wrong. There were simply not enough jobs for everyone. But at least Helena had tried, done what she could to help one unemployed person, although Hugh would probably never know.

"What's it like?" she asked dully.

"What's what like?" asked Mrs. Boyd.

"Ynysceiber," said Helena.

"Is that how it's pronounced?"

In the station cafeteria Helena had written it on a scrap of paper. In-is-ky-ber, the girl had said. That was where the colliery was, Helena had told her, where her father worked as manager and Hugh could have a job if he wanted one.

"Ynysceiber," the girl repeated. "I'll tell him, miss."

And she had not seemed dishonest.

"The house is wonderful," said Mrs. Boyd. "Parquet floors throughout, and a landscaped garden. All you could wish for, really. And the views are splendid."

"But what's Ynysceiber like?"

Her mother shrugged.

And dabbed her mouth with a paper napkin.

"It's just a place," she said.

"It's awful, isn't it?"

"It's not quite what we're used to," Mrs. Boyd admitted.

"You mean it's a dump?" said Helena.

"But the house is wonderful," Mrs. Boyd repeated.

But there was more to life than a house, thought Helena.

You could be a millionaire and live in a palace, and still be miserable and lonely. More than ever now she hated South Wales, and hated the British Mining Company for transferring them there.

"It's no use moping," said Mrs. Boyd. "What cannot be cured must be endured, so we may as well make the best of it. We'll go and buy something new to cheer ourselves up, shall we?"

Helena shrugged.

There was a term for that.

It was called compensation buying.

And the effects were always temporary.

■   ■   ■

"See you in the morning," said Hugh.

"Early," said Colin.

Hugh nodded and looked to Flutey. "You made up your mind yet?"

"No," said Flutey.

"You've got one more night then," said Colin.

"And we'll call for you anyway," said Hugh.

They parted outside the terraced house in Swindon Street, and Hugh maneuvered the empty handcart up the side alley and into the backyard. It was a strange feeling, knowing he was leaving and might never return. Things impressed themselves on his vision, demanding to be remembered . . . moss between the flagstones, shoots of mint in a plastic tub, and his father's trousers hung to dry on a string clothesline.

It was the same when he entered the house . . . indelible impressions of linoleum tiles worn to holes, kitchen cupboards with broken doors, a knob missing from the stove, and his mother's face. She was chopping cabbage for the evening meal. Her eyes, gray as his own, with crow's-feet at the corners, glanced at him indifferently. And lines of weariness were etched around her mouth.

"You're home early," she said.

Hugh grinned. "Guess what, Mam."

"Been another riot, has there?"

"No," said Hugh. "Me, Flutey, and Colin are going to get a job. Working in a coal mine . . . up the valley in Ynysceiber."

"How did you hear about that?" asked Mrs. Davies.

"From Helena," said Hugh.

"What's *she* got to do with it?"

"Sent me a message, she did. It's all fixed up, see? And she didn't forget us after all. Three hundred and fifty ecu a week, that's what I'll be getting!"

No one spoke. His mother continued chopping the cabbage, and in the sitting room the newspaper rustled. The tap dripped and rain tapped softly on the windowpane.

"You'll be leaving then?" said Mrs. Davies.

"Tomorrow morning," said Hugh.

There was another silence.

His mother peeled an onion and unwrapped the minced meat, pointedly ignored him. It was as if he had done something wrong . . . been arrested in the street for indecent exposure.

"I thought you'd be pleased," said Hugh.

"Excuse me," said his mother.

She hunted under the sink for saucepans.

And in the sitting room the newspaper rustled again.

"I don't understand," said Hugh.

"We'll be losing your benefits," said Mrs. Davies.

"Is that all you care about?"

"To those in our position fifty ecu is a lot of money."

"So I'll send you sixty a week to make up for it."

"I suppose we could take in a lodger."

"I'm going away, Mam!"

"Yes," said his mother.

His father came from the sitting room.

He was grim and unsmiling, not looking at Hugh.

"I'm going out," he said.

"You don't have to do that," said Mrs. Davies.

"Heard what I said, didn't you?"

"It's not the boy's fault, Mervyn."

"I'm going out anyway!"

"Keep your dinner hot, shall I?"

He left without answering.

Mrs. Davies shrugged.

"What's wrong with *him*?" asked Hugh.

His mother turned to him.

"Not thinking, are you Hugh? Not thinking how your Da must feel. He is unemployed for fifteen years now, and you are getting a job. But he is your father, see? It ought to be him you are looking up to, not the other way about."

"I can't help the way things are!" said Hugh.

"I am knowing that well enough," said Mrs. Davies. "It is good you are finding a future for yourself. But you will be succeeding where your father has failed, and for him that is a bitter pill to swallow. You go shouting your mouth off like you did, and you may as well be giving him a kick in the teeth!"

Hugh stared at her and understood.

She was protecting his father from his own uselessness.
Sad for both of them, he went upstairs to pack his bags.

■　■　■

Helena sat on the white-painted windowsill of her new bedroom. Drizzling cloud obscured the view. All she had seen
of Ynysceiber was a vague impression as the car passed
through . . . wet streets, endless terraces of houses and
closed-down shops, everything gray and shadowy. There
was a supermarket and a newsstand, one hardware store,
several pubs, several secondhand shops, and a biweekly market in the parking lot by the river, Mrs. Boyd had said. It
was dismal, thought Helena. And Highview House was no
consolation.

It was high on the hill in splendid isolation, not a farm
anymore although it retained some of the original features:
the inglenook fireplace in the parlor, beamed ceilings, and a
small back staircase leading to the attics that had once been
the servants' quarters. Everything else was new . . . paint
and plaster and parquet floors, a solid-fuel cooking stove in
the kitchen, oak units and marbled work surfaces, double-
glazed windows, a downstairs bathroom and patio doors.
Radiators sang softly, and the wall-to-wall carpet in Helena's
bedroom was tastefully woven with birds and flowers in
pastel colors. White built-in closets were scrolled with gold,
and a display of pink silk flowers was arranged on the dressing table.

Downstairs, voices seemed strange and echoey.
Cooking smells wafted from the kitchen.
And the telephone rang.
Nothing had anything to do with Helena.
It was as if she had arrived in a foreign country . . . an

70

unknown place, an unknown land, an unknown household. Routines and customs had been established without her. Even Angharad, the daily domestic help, belonged in a way Helena did not. The loneliness depressed her, and her sense of alienation grew with every passing minute.

"Helena!"

"What?"

"Have you finished unpacking?"

"Not yet."

"Your father telephoned. He'll be late home, so dinner will be ready in fifteen minutes. You don't need to change."

"I wasn't going to," muttered Helena.

There was no one to change for, no one to see her, no one to impress . . . just two boring weeks to be spent with her mother, in a house in the middle of nowhere. She stared, morosely, through the window. Rain and cloud drifted across the garden . . . the expanse of rolled earth that would soon become a lawn, and the flower borders beyond it freshly planted with twigs of roses, ornamental shrubs, and trees. Surrounding it all, inescapable and unclimbable, was a three-meter-high security fence topped with barbed wire.

And what kept people out kept Helena in. Locked gates separated her from the rest of humanity, as if she were a criminal. This was not a house, she thought. It was a prison! She had no home . . . just a pain inside her, a need, a longing for something she did not quite understand. Would that feeling change if Hugh came? she wondered. Would Ynysceiber become suddenly beautiful along with her life?

6

Early in the morning Hugh left with twenty ecu in his pocket, a pack of jam sandwiches and his things in the handcart in two shopping bags. No one waved good-bye. His mother remained in the kitchen minding her own feelings, and his father was sleeping off a hangover. And maybe, in his mind, he had left them long ago, so he felt no grief.

It was a good day for a journey. The air was crisp and clear. Daffodils bloomed in front gardens of the housing development, and the door to Number Eighty-nine opened as he reached the gate. Colin, Dilys and their mother came hurrying down the path with their arms full of things. Old coats and blankets, cutlery, crockery and saucepans, spare shoes and a battered suitcase, bottles of water and a lunch box, were dumped in the handcart. Tears ran down Mrs. Williams' face.

"Got all you need, have you?"

"All we can carry," said Colin.

"No need for you to cry, Mam," said Dilys.

"You look after them, *cariad.*"

"That's why I'm going," said Dilys.

"You coming with us?" asked Hugh.

"She insisted," said Colin.

"A new life for all of you," said Mrs. Williams.

And she laughed through her tears, hugged them and kissed them, hugged Hugh too. The two younger children waved from the doorway. And then they were leaving, three of them together, silent with their own emotions, the hand-cart trundling through the early-morning streets to Flutey's house.

He had made up his mind . . . was waiting on the door-step, his things packed in a tartan bag. And his mother beside him, dark skinned and huge, laughing and crying with all her grief and gladness . . . his father, small and slight and graying, solemnly shaking their hands and wishing them luck. A young brother and sister pressed their noses to a bedroom window, watched as they rearranged the handcart, not understanding Flutey was going away.

"You write to me, son," his father said quietly.

"You let us know how you are," said his mother.

Flutey blinked away his tears.

And no one looked back as they headed into the morning.

Sunlight and silence were everywhere about them . . . new leaves unfurling on the elder bush that grew through the chapel windows . . . grass and nettles heaving up the steps. A blackbird sang in a nearby garden, and a distant clock chimed six. And the streets were empty, Cardiff still sleeping as they passed through. The broken windows of office blocks towered above them, and sparrows squabbled in the burned-out buildings of the city center. And a train whistled behind them as they turned past the castle and the civic center and headed toward the northern suburbs.

"Where are we going?" asked Colin.

"Ynysceiber," said Hugh.

"But where is Ynysceiber?"

"Out past Pontypridd?"

"You mean you don't know?" asked Flutey.

"Not exactly," said Hugh.

"We could be on the wrong road!" said Dilys.

"No," said Hugh. "This is the way to Pontypridd, all right."

A man on a bicycle, with a knapsack on his shoulder, rode toward the center of the city. Another man, stoned or drunk or homeless, slept in a doorway. And a group of women with colored scarves knotted around their heads waited at a bus stop. An orange double-decker came rumbling toward them. Cardiff, it said, as if in all the world there were no other place.

"I hope we're doing the right thing," Colin said worriedly.

"We couldn't turn down the chance of a real job," said Flutey.

"And without us Mam might marry Bill," said Dilys.

"Is that why you came?" asked Hugh.

"Partly," said Dilys.

"There'll be no job for you in a coal mine, girlie."

"What I earn will be more than enough for me and Dilys," said Colin. "I'll make sure she doesn't want for nothing."

"We'll look out for each other," said Hugh.

"All for one and one for all," declared Dilys.

74

"That's right," said Hugh. "And whose turn is it to shove the handcart?"

■ ■ ■

The suburbs seemed endless . . . streets, shops, houses, parks, hospitals, going on and on through each successive suburb. And along the main road the traffic flow increased . . . bicycles, buses, delivery vans, and a few private cars, all heading in the opposite direction. North Road changed to Merthyr Road, and changed again to Northern Avenue, until finally they came to fields and a highway junction, a shadowy bridge beneath a six-lane highway that was no longer used. Vast rusting road signs indicated the way to Pontypridd.

"There you are," said Hugh. "What did I tell you?"

"We're on the right road," said Flutey.

"And look at that castle," said Dilys. "There's fantastic!"

Ahead of them the valley narrowed. The road, the railway, and the River Taff beside it passed through a gorge of wooded hills to an unseen land beyond. A castle guarded the approaches . . . not ruinous stones, a remnant of some past historical era, but all intact, towered and turreted as if from a fairy tale. All the fields and copses, and the river at its feet, must once have belonged to it, thought Hugh. People too, owned by the lord who owned the castle, and bound to him like slaves. It was hard to imagine such inescapable servitude, but its shadow touched him as he passed beneath.

"I wish we could live somewhere like that," said Dilys.

"Why?" asked Hugh.

"We could grow vegetables and fish in the river," said Flutey.

"Everywhere's owned," said Hugh. "There's too many

people, and not enough land. All been claimed, it has, and parceled out, and nowhere left for the likes of us. Born too late we are, see?"

Dilys sighed.

And Colin, pushing the handcart, paused to look back.

"Are you lot coming to Ynysceiber or returning to Cardiff?"

"We're coming," said Hugh.

And they were not the only ones.

Ahead of them, where the road straightened, they saw a bald-headed man in a gray raincoat carrying a black holdall. And ahead of him was a family, with children, pushing a baby carriage . . . and others beyond, traveling singly, or in pairs, or in small groups joined together. The divided highway, designed for twentieth-century traffic, held a small exodus of people.

"Where are they all going?" asked Dilys.

"They must have heard there are jobs," said Colin.

"How?" asked Flutey.

"Same way as we heard?" said Hugh.

And a man called Di confirmed it.

He sat on the side of the road, by the entrance to the Taffs Well industrial park, eating sandwiches. He was fit and fortyish, with a natural tonsure of lank brown hair. Blue eyes twinkled and there were lines of laughter at the corners of his mouth. It had never occurred to him to want to be a miner, he said. But a girl in the cafeteria at the Cardiff Station had told his daughter there were vacancies in the pit at Ynysceiber.

"So here I am," said Di.

"You left your family?" asked Dilys.

"I'll send for them, see? Soon as I know for sure I've got a job and have found a place to settle."

A coal train chuffed down the valley. Grass grew in the road through the cracks in the asphalt. And the empty factories behind them were silent in the midday heat. Above, and on either side, small fields were angled into the hillsides and a few sheep grazed. Hugh massaged his feet that were hurting from the walk.

"How far *is* Ynysceiber?" he asked Di.

"We ought to be there by nightfall," Di replied.

They traveled together after that, caught up and joined with a young married couple who were also making for Ynysceiber. David carried a guitar and suitcase, and Glenda, his wife, was five months pregnant. They had been living with in-laws for the past two years and were looking to begin a new life together. David's uncle ran a corner shop in Splott, which was how they had heard about the vacancies in the pit.

"He didn't say how many," said Glenda.

"They could all be gone by the time we get there," said David.

"I can't walk any faster," said Glenda.

"No hurry anyway," Di said cheerfully. "They won't be interviewing until tomorrow, will they?"

"And my feet are killing me," said Hugh.

They walked all afternoon, ate supper by the river in Pontypridd, lingered between the gray terraced houses and the water. Glenda had a backache, and there was not much left of the soles of Hugh's sneakers. Shadows lengthened as they began to walk the last long miles to Ynysceiber. And the fear of unemployment followed them, the memory of Cardiff and a lifetime of degradation to which they might have to return.

■ ■ ■

It was past seven o'clock when Mr. Boyd returned from the colliery. Angharad had gone home, and Helena and her mother had dined already before the car pulled in. The evening sun slanted through the landing window and shadows of the cow barn, converted into workshops and garaging, lay long and deep across the graveled farmyard. Gnats danced beneath the trees by the barn. Helena paused, about to go downstairs, then heard their voices in the kitchen.

"I've had half of Cardiff asking for work!" said her father.

"I assumed you'd be home on time as you didn't telephone," said Mrs. Boyd.

"Trainloads! Busloads! By the hundreds!" said Mr. Boyd.

"We waited dinner as long as we could."

"They'd heard some kind of rumor," said Mr. Boyd.

"You'd better have a shower, dear, and change your clothes."

"I had to turn them all away."

"I thought Sir Gerald was intending to reopen a second colliery?"

"He is," said Mr. Boyd.

"Then surely you'll be needing more labor before long?"

"Not until next year," said Mr. Boyd. "And then we've no need to look beyond the valley. There are enough unemployed in the area to run half a dozen pits! I don't know how these things start, I really don't. All those hopes dashed in a single day. And how many more are still on their way here? I'd like to ring somebody's neck!"

"I'll pour you a whiskey and soda," said Mrs. Boyd.

Helena retreated back upstairs and closed her bedroom door. Terrible feelings shot through her, she thought she might be responsible . . . a careless word in the station cafeteria spread throughout the city. But the message she had given the girl was specifically for Hugh. She had made certain of that, made her repeat his name . . . Hugh Davies, who lived in Splott.

She went to the window and looked out. Beyond the high mesh fence the view was clear down the valley as far as she could see . . . small terraced houses built into the hillside, darkening with shadow, and no telling where Ynysceiber ended and the next town began. She could see the river at the bottom, and the railway line beside it, and the pale ribbon of road with shapes small as ants moving along it. Half of Cardiff, her father had said, had come here looking for work. There would be hopes dashed tomorrow as well. But it was not Helena's fault. No way had she begun the rumor, she decided.

She switched on the bedside lamp and picked up the book she was reading. She had bought it in Penarth, a historical romance set in Victorian times about a servant girl and a rich man's son. Escapist literature, the English teacher would have called it. Not the sort of book Helena was encouraged to read at school. But it was better than the assigned books she was studying for exams, far more exciting than Thomas Hardy and Jane Austen.

Annie was swept into his arms.
His lips were hot, passionate, kissing her throat.
"Oh, what shall we do?" she whispered.
"They want me to marry Lady Melissa," Alistair groaned.

And if Hugh came to Ynysceiber, thought Helena, she would be in the same position as Alistair. Her mother would want her to marry a banker or an insurance broker, not someone from a deprived background. Or maybe Hugh would not fancy her anyway? She went to the mirror and studied her face. She was too pale. She needed some color in her cheeks and around her eyes . . . blusher and lip gloss and mascara. She made herself up, pinned back her hair in a sophisticated style, added a pair of dangling earrings and gazed at the woman she had become.

"Helena! Your father's home!"

Her mother's voice disturbed her.

She heard it as a summons that had to be obeyed.

And she went downstairs.

Mrs. Boyd stared at her.

"Are you going somewhere, Helena?"

Then she felt slightly ridiculous, realized that if Hugh came to Ynysceiber, he would be coming to work, not to see her. For her nothing would ever change. She was imprisoned in Highview House, and going nowhere until she returned to Kent.

■　■　■

It was dark when they arrived in Ynysceiber. They were weary from traveling, and needing somewhere to sleep. Orange lights shone on the closed doors of houses, and the road led steeply down toward the valley floor. Shops in the main street were mostly boarded up. But there was music and laughter coming from a nearby pub. Di and David went to inquire, and the others waited, their hopes eroded by tiredness, their conversation long ago lapsed into silence. Dilys had blisters on her hands from pushing the handcart. Glenda's backache was worse, and Hugh's feet were raw.

"You'll have to soak them in salt water," said Dilys.

A few moments later Di and David returned.

There was no work at the colliery, they said.

And there was nowhere to sleep either.

"Unless we've got twenty-five ecu each for lodgings," said Di.

"We've come all this way for nothing!" said David.

"Bloody hell!" said Colin.

"What are we going to do?" asked Flutey.

"I can't walk any farther!" wailed Glenda.

"So much for Lady Helena!" Dilys said angrily.

"Who's Lady Helena?" asked Di.

"She sent the message to say there were jobs here," said Dilys.

"You mean the girl in the station cafeteria?"

"Helena Boyd!" said Dilys. "The lying cow!"

"There's got to be some mistake," said Hugh.

"Well," said Di, "there's nothing we can do tonight, is there? Leave it till the morning, shall we? Find somewhere to sleep and then decide?"

"We could squat," said Hugh.

"You mean break in somewhere?" asked David.

"There were several boarded-up houses a little way back," said Colin.

"Or the derelict chapel," said Dilys.

"Whichever's easiest," said Di.

"I wish I'd never left home," muttered Flutey.

"Aw, come on," said Di. "This is a big adventure, boyo. Let's not give up before we have to. We'll go and find somewhere to sleep, then look for a fries stand, see? Get some warm food inside us."

Colin turned the handcart.

"I'm not sure we've got enough money for fries."

"Not to worry," said Di. "I've got a few ecu to spare. I'll treat us, see? Providing no one's greedy."

Weary, dispirited, they trudged back along the road.

And the closed doors of Ynysceiber did not welcome them.

■ ■ ■

The house was an end terrace. A For Sale sign was attached to the front of it and its boarded-up windows overlooked the street. But the door was dead-bolt locked, refusing to yield.

"What if someone comes?" asked Glenda.

"We're not doing any harm," said Dilys.

"Breaking and entering is still a crime," said Flutey.

"Maybe we'd better try the Methodist chapel," said David.

"At least it's not private property," said Glenda.

"I'll just try round the back," said Di.

"I'll come with you," said Hugh.

"And *we'll* wait somewhere less obvious," said Colin.

He pushed the handcart on up the hill.

"*Nos da,*" said Glenda.

"And don't be too long," said Dilys.

By moonlight and starlight Hugh followed Di around the side of the house. A gate tied with string led into a concrete yard, and there was a high retaining wall built into the hillside. The house was L-shaped; a kitchen with a bathroom over it backed onto the house next door and offered them privacy. But again the door was dead-bolt locked, impossible to open.

"It'll have to be the window," said Di.

He took a penknife from his pocket and levered away the protective plywood, then inserted the blade between the sashes, released the catch, and pried the window open.

"You done this before?" asked Hugh.

"Once or twice," Di admitted. "I'm not proud of it but it's one way of making ends meet . . . a bit of petty pilfering. Not what I want for my kids, though. Now go and fetch the others."

"Right," said Hugh.

He returned to the street.

On up the hill, with the handcart, the others lingered beneath an orange light as a group of men went past them. Drunken voices were loud and abusive in the night's silence.

"That's right!"

"You bug off back to Cardiff!"

"We don't want no outsiders moving in here!"

"What jobs there are going are for us, see?"

"There is nothing for you in Ynysceiber."

"And we don't want no blacks here, either."

Hugh watched and waited.

People peered through the curtains of nearby houses. But no one ventured out and no one answered, not even Dilys, until finally the men grew tired of being ignored and drifted away. The streetlights shone on Glenda's tears as Hugh approached.

"You all right, are you?"

"Did you hear them?" asked Colin.

"I heard," said Hugh.

"Bastards!" said Dilys.

"I hate Ynysceiber," sobbed Glenda.

"Maybe we ought to leave?" said Flutey.

"Not tonight," said Hugh.

"Di found a way in?" asked David.

"Round the back," said Hugh.

He led the way, and the others followed. The dark back-yard was safer than the street, but the house itself was hardly inviting. Di had removed the door from its hinges, and beyond the gap of the doorway the inside was as black as pitch. It smelled too, musty and unlived in, and the stone walls exuded a chill. Hugh's voice echoed.

"Are you in there, Di?"

"Keep your voice down!" hissed Dilys.

"We don't want trouble with the neighbors," said David.

"Leastways not tonight," said Glenda.

Hugh shuffled forward, groped his way along the wall.

Then a match flared in a cupboard in the hallway. "Let there be light," announced Di.

And he switched on the electric light.

"Do you really think that's wise?" asked Colin.

"Someone might see," Flutey said nervously.

Hugh left them to argue, wandered through the empty rooms and up the stairs. It was a strange feeling, taking possession of the house, almost like taking possession of his own life, as if he had a right. And maybe he did . . . the right to clothes and food and shelter . . . and here was his shelter. No crime committed in the claiming of it, no intention to damage, no one unhoused because of him.

Two rooms upstairs, two down, and bathroom and kitchen.

The back bedroom window was not boarded.

He opened it and leaned out.

Light from the kitchen fell across the yard. Flutey and Dilys were unloading the handcart, and a dark expanse of hillside rose above them, a wilderness of rocks and gorse and brambles, grass made pale by the moonlight. And high on the hill's crest were trees against the skyline, buildings that might be barns and cowsheds surrounding a large farmhouse. Its lights shone like lodestars above the valley.

He felt the night's cold rising from the earth beneath him. He smelled the unknown air that stirred his blood. It was as if something called to him, out there in the bleat of sheep, and the hoot of owls, and the heavy tread of boots along the street. Then there were footsteps on the floor behind him and he turned his head.

"It's good here," said Hugh.

"David and Glenda aren't staying after tonight," said Colin.

"Feels right, it does."

"And Flutey says he's going back to Cardiff."

"Almost like a pattern, the way things happened. As if it was meant."

"You're not listening," said Colin.

"And you're not seeing, are you?"

"Everything's gone wrong, Hugh!"

"No," said Hugh. "That's what I'm telling you. Everything's going to be all right."

7

The house faced east across the valley, and morning sunlight shone through the window when Hugh awoke. He put on his clothes, stepped over the bodies on the floor that were still sleeping, and went downstairs. The kitchen was in shadow, and there was nothing to eat except the stale crust of a sandwich. Breakfast, thought Hugh, was the first priority. He shifted away the barricade of door and went outside.

The air smelled of spring, and there were clumps of primroses growing on the bank behind the house, celandines on the empty lot to the side of it. Small birds fluted amid the gorse, and the house on the hill was not a farm but some kind of renovated mansion, beech trees around it showing a tinge of green. The town was before him . . . steep streets going down to the river and the railway line, and the main road beyond it. Gray slate roofs reflected a sheen of light in every direction, an urban sprawl between the green hills rising. Or maybe they were not so green. Under the surface Hugh could see the ancient darkness of coal dust. And to the north the whole hillside was black with recent slag heaps. He could hear the clatter of the winding wheel, the clank of machinery, and the soft shunting of a train.

It was all Ynysceiber had to depend on, the only work there was in all the length of the valley. Nothing else but the colliery . . . no other industry, no land fit for cultivation, no option. No wonder they guarded it so jealously against incomers, thought Hugh. The unemployment level must be worse than it was in Splott. He read the signs: a used condom in the gutter, dried vomit on the sidewalk, scraps of straws and silver paper used for snorting drugs, and beat music blasting from the open window of a nearby house . . . the same degradation he had been hoping to escape from. And there were no jobs, of course. What had given hope to half the unemployed of Cardiff was a misunderstanding, something Helena had arranged for Hugh and no one else.

He saw, in the sunlight at the corner of the street, the family with the baby carriage who had yesterday walked the road ahead of him, turned despondently toward home. He was responsible for that, he thought, the double journey and all their disappointment. He was responsible for Glenda and David, Di and Colin and Dilys and Flutey . . . people he knew, and did not know, who had come there because of him. Their lives and losses lay heavy in his conscience and he could offer them nothing.

The doorbell jangled as he entered the shop.

And a man wearing a grimed apron came from the back room.

"*Bore da,*" said the man. "A lovely morning, it is."

87

"For some," said Hugh.

"You from Cardiff, are you?"

"Splott," said Hugh.

"Wasting your time coming here, boy."

"You refusing to serve me?"

"I mean looking for work," said the man. "There aren't any vacancies, see?"

"So we've been told," said Hugh.

"My wife can be making sandwiches for your journey back . . . fish paste or cheese . . . reasonable prices."

Hugh nodded.

"Remember that, I will, when we're ready to go."

"Something I can get for you now, is there?"

Hugh ordered a few essentials . . . egg and milk powder, tea and breakfast cereal scooped from tubs into brown paper bags. A slab of margarine came wrapped in waxed paper, and two loaves of bread and two large cans of sardines in tomato sauce were carefully packed in a paper shopping bag.

"You're not by yourself then?" observed the shopkeeper.

"We are seven of us," said Hugh.

"Someone needs shooting," said the shopkeeper.

"Who's that?" asked Hugh.

"Whoever started the rumor. Wicked, it was. Absolutely wicked! All these people coming here for nothing. You're staying at the chapel, I suppose? And is there anything else you are needing?"

Hugh had only three ecu left to last until his first wage packet. All for one and one for all, Dilys had said. But if she and Colin and Flutey returned to Cardiff, then how would he manage? No, thought Hugh, they were together whatever happened, and there had to be something he could do.

"Keep your pecker up," said the shopkeeper.

"Yes," said Hugh. "I will lift up mine eyes unto the hills from whence cometh my help. And whose is that bloody great house up there?"

"That'll be Griffith's farm," said the shopkeeper. "Highview House, they call it now. It is belonging to Mr. Boyd, who is managing the colliery."

"I thought he lived in Penarth?"

"He and his wife were moving in a month ago now."

"And presumably Helena's with them?"

"I am not knowing them personally," said the shopkeeper.

"Thank you anyway," said Hugh.

The man nodded.

"There is a bus going to Cardiff once a week," he said. "Thursday morning at a quarter to nine. For five ecu you can save yourself the walk, see?"

"Thank you," Hugh said again.

But he had not given up, not yet.

■　■　■

"Well," said Glenda, "that's something positive."

"At least we won't have to walk back to Cardiff," said David.

"I'd like to kill that stupid Helena!" said Dilys.

"She should have made things clear in the first place!" said Colin.

"If she had," said Hugh, "none of us would have come here."

"It's all right for you," said Colin.

"You've got a guaranteed job," said Flutey.

"But is it worth more than friendship?" asked Hugh.

"That's for you to decide," Dilys said primly.

89

They sat on the floor in the dining room, the window board removed to let in the light. Midmorning sun was bright in the backyard, its Midas touch turning all things to gold. But the truth had depressed them, and except for Hugh they had no reason to stay in Ynysceiber.

"I think we should go to the mine anyway," said Di.

"What's the point?" asked Colin. "We know there aren't any jobs."

"You've got nothing to lose," said Glenda.

"It's possible Mr. Boyd might make an exception," said David.

"Not for me, he won't," said Flutey.

"Just because you're black . . ."

"You heard what was said last night. . . ."

"Flaming morons!" said Dilys.

"We'll all be black down in a coal mine," said Di.

But Flutey shook his head.

"There might be another way," said Hugh.

"Like what?" asked David.

"I could pay Helena a visit."

"What the hell for?" asked Colin.

"Well," said Hugh, "to my way of thinking we might be able to come to some kind of arrangement. For keeping our traps shut, see? Wouldn't want her Da to know she's been indiscreet, now would she?"

"That's blackmail!" said David.

"Kinder than giving her to Dilys," said Hugh.

"You wouldn't do it anyway!" said Dilys.

"Wouldn't I?" said Hugh.

"It's just another excuse to go and see her!"

"You wait and see," said Hugh.

"We'll be waiting all right," said Colin.

"Twenty-four hours for the frigging bus!" said Dilys.

He left with Di and David, who decided to go to the colliery anyway; but beyond the corner shop, where the hill slope steepened and the houses petered out, he was on his own. A lane led up to Highview House, bordered by dry stone walls that kept the sheep from straying into town. He walked parallel to the street below, looking down on the gray terraces of houses. He could see the empty lot with celandines, and the small backyard . . . Dilys and Glenda arguing with a group of women who had gathered outside the gate. Raised voices reached him, mingled with sounds from the valley, and just for a moment he was tempted to turn back. But whatever the trouble, it was nothing Dilys could not handle, so he continued on up the lane.

A high security fence, topped with barbed wire, surrounded the house, and locked gates confronted him where the road ended. Beyond were extensive gardens newly laid to lawn, and a graveled drive that curved past trees and a hay barn of what had once been a farmyard. And to one side of the gates was a box containing a bell push and an intercom that would connect him to whoever answered it.

Hugh hesitated.

Quite simply he had no cause to contact Helena, except to thank her for a job he had not yet got and was of two minds about whether to accept anyway. If the others returned to Cardiff, he was not sure he wanted to stay in Ynysceiber. Three hundred and fifty ecu a week would hardly compensate for the loss of them in his life. And was money really what he wanted? Dilys was right, of course. It was not in his nature to blackmail Helena.

He shrugged and turned away.

And he felt again what he had felt the night before: something calling in the sunlight among the rocks and gorse and dead brown heather, tugging his heartstrings and urging him to go. It was a need, or a longing, he did not know which. He only knew he would find it, out there in the wild high land, whatever it was he was seeking.

"Nice day for a walk anyway," said Hugh.

■ ■ ■

Over the valley the morning lay clear and bright. And that made it worse, thought Helena.

Her mother's words echoed in her head.

"Of course you're to blame! How else could this rumor have started? Shooting your mouth off in the station cafeteria to all and sundry! Totally irresponsible! And even if you didn't and that boy did . . . you are still the instigator. You ought to have more sense, Helena! And God knows what Sir Gerald Fraser will think if he ever gets to hear of it! Nepotism is hardly an attractive asset in one of the company's employees! Your father could lose his job because of this!"

Helena blinked back her tears and hated. She hated the place, and hated her mother, and hated Hugh. It was his fault she was in trouble. All she had done was send him a message, and that had been clear enough. The sound of his voice shocked her.

"Morning, Miss Helena."

She turned her head.

His eyes were gray as the sea at Penarth.

And her mind was gripped by a terrible confusion.

"Are you all right?" he asked her.

"No," said Helena. "I'm not all right."

"Do anything to help, can I?"

92

"What have you been saying?" she demanded.

"Pardon?" said Hugh.

"It was private," said Helena. "Private between you and me. You didn't have to go blabbing it all over Cardiff!"

"I'm not quite with you, Miss Helena."

"Mommy's absolutely furious!"

"About what?" asked Hugh.

"All those people coming here looking for jobs!" Helena said bitterly. "My father had to turn them all away! And if Sir Gerald Fraser gets to hear . . . That message was for you, Hugh. You didn't need to spread it about!"

Hugh stared at her, unflinching eyes fixed on her own.

Somewhere a bird called.

And water trickled between the stones.

"Beg pardon, Miss Helena, but the message I received wasn't exactly clear, see? Work, said the girl, and not just to me. Her Da's up at the colliery right now having words with your Da. Nice man, he is. Walked all the way from Cardiff with him, we did. Now, if you'll excuse me . . ."

He turned on his heel, headed toward the open hillside beyond the crags. Helena scrambled to her feet and went running after him. Sheep scattered in all directions, and the wind snatched away her voice.

"Don't go, Hugh! Please don't go!"

He stopped and looked back at her.

She was aware of the mess of her hair, her unbecoming duffle coat and boots. Aware of a need inside her, acute as pain, for someone to care and someone to talk to. And what did he see when he looked at her? A rich English bitch, snobbish and awful, accusing him of something he had not done?

"I'm sorry," Helena said wretchedly.

93

"Apology accepted, miss."

"It's just that . . . Mommy wasn't too pleased, that's all."

"Tear strips off you, did she?"

"She was horrid," said Helena.

"Go for a walk, shall we? Talk things over?"

She stared at him, hardly believing.

"Got something better to do, have you?"

"No," said Helena.

"Best foot forward then," said Hugh.

"But where will we go?"

"Does it matter?" he asked her.

They set out together over the hill toward the wide sky, the wind in their faces. Sheep-bitten turf was springy beneath their feet, and the sunlight glittered on the gorse and grass, on the dampness of stones and the mounds of dead bracken. The valley was out of sight, and the air smelled of spring, and Helena felt new and strange, touched by a thing she did not understand, both glad and afraid. And Hugh was beside her, his eyes fixed on the distances, as if he had forgotten she was there.

"I never dreamed there was so much space," he said.

"And all of it useless," said Helena.

"You could walk forever and never meet a soul."

"And if you fell in a bog, no one would find you."

"Puts you in your place, it does."

"It's awfully bleak," said Helena.

"Boundless and magical," said Hugh.

"You actually like it?"

"Don't you?"

"No," said Helena. "And I've never set out to go nowhere before."

"What about your life?" he asked her.

"What about it?" she said.

"You going somewhere there, are you? Got it all mapped out, destination in mind?"

"Mommy wants me to go into banking."

"But what do *you* want?" asked Hugh.

She hesitated, suddenly realizing that she did not know, not really. The plans she had made seemed somehow meaningless . . . meaningless her years in Kent, her aims, her ambitions, cramming for exams. What did she want? he asked. She tried to think. An apartment in Kensington? Vacations abroad? Or this moment now, walking in the sunlight with him? She glanced at him, and some unexpected joy burbled up inside her. There were some things money could never buy.

"I'm so glad you came," she told him.

"I won't be staying," he replied.

■ ■ ■

Then it was a kind of death she felt, everything beautiful snatched away before she even knew what it was. And Hugh became a stranger, someone she had never met before. She noticed his shoes falling to pieces, holes in his jeans, and the torn pockets of his parka. With one week's wages he could rig himself out. She did not understand him, did not understand how he could turn down all she offered.

He tried to explain.

They were friends, he said, Colin and Dilys and Flutey . . . Glenda and David and Di . . . closer than family because he had not been born with them but chosen them. And it was his fault they had come to Ynysceiber. He had believed they would all get jobs and live and work together. And how could he accept a position at the colliery where they would be refused?

"I don't see why not," said Helena.

"It's leaving them behind," said Hugh.

"If they're your friends, they'll be glad for you, surely?"

"But I can't be glad to see them return to Cardiff with nothing, can I? And where will it leave me anyway?"

"It will leave you three hundred and fifty ecu a week better off, for one thing."

"And bereft of my own kind," said Hugh.

"I don't understand what you mean."

"We are together, see?"

"No, I don't see."

"If what I earned could keep them here . . ."

"They can claim welfare, can't they?"

"Dilys and Colin and Flutey are under age."

"But the others aren't."

"You have to be living in a place for twelve months before you can claim."

"So you're willing to turn down the greatest chance of your life . . ."

"If it's a chance for me and no chance for them, then I have to refuse it. Why should I be singled out to enjoy what they cannot? I am no different from them, no more deserving."

"That's crazy, Hugh!"

"It's how I feel, Miss Helena."

"Don't keep calling me that!"

"It's how I feel," Hugh repeated.

"So what about *my* feelings?"

"It's not personal, Helena."

"Of course it's personal! Why else would I have put myself to this kind of bother? I did it for you, Hugh. Don't you realize that?"

He stared across the uplands.

Cotton grass danced in the wind and a bird called, sadly from far away. And he, too, was far away . . . belonging to a different world, stubborn and unreachable and full of strange ideas, turning his back out of loyalty to others. Helena did not understand him and never would, but neither could she let him leave.

"How many are there?" she asked.

"How many what?" asked Hugh.

"How many of your friends want jobs?"

"Four," said Hugh.

"I'll speak to Daddy then."

He turned to her.

There was a softness in his eyes that disturbed a tumult of feelings. And a softness in his voice.

"You'd do that for me?"

"Yes," said Helena.

"Why?" he asked her.

"Don't you know?" she said.

And in that moment they changed each other's lives.

8

Time did not matter, for the hills were timeless, and Helena knew she would never forget that day with Hugh. It was as if, through her connection with him, she became connected to the land itself. She saw what he saw . . . cloud shadows chasing across the moors, and the subtly changing colors of the landscape. She felt the power of earth and stones and tumbling water . . . the magic he had mentioned, and the bleak wild beauty. The air was alive with lark songs and her own laughter. She shared a chocolate bar from her pocket, and he shared the moss and ferns and stands of rushes, a clump of saxifrage flowering in a rocky crevice.

"This is what really matters," said Hugh.

"How do you mean?" asked Helena.

"In Cardiff . . . in Ynysceiber . . . we're involved in a kind of madness, see? But here everything's sane."

"No one could live up here," said Helena.

"We could build a hut out of stones," said Hugh.

"And what would we eat?"

"Bilberries and rabbits."

"And make our bed out of heather, I suppose?"

"Be nice, it would."

"Now I know you're crazy," said Helena.

They sat on a rock with the stream beneath them. Maybe it would be nice, she thought, living up here with Hugh, cut off from everyone and not caring about the rest of the world. But it was only a dream. Soon they would go home, and all of this would seem unreal, no more than a memory in her mind. Already other things intruded . . . the chocolate that had made her thirsty, and the knowledge she had missed her lunch.

"Is the water safe to drink?" she asked.

"Direct from heaven," said Hugh.

"But is it safe?"

"Try it, shall we?"

They skidded down the bank and knelt among the stones. The water was icy in Helena's cupped hands, the taste of it pure and cold and nutty, like no water she had ever drunk before.

"It's wonderful," she said.

"Except for the sheep shit," said Hugh.

"You told me it was safe!"

"And bird droppings and minnow farts," said Hugh.

"You told me . . ."

"Ever read an analysis of Welsh water, girlie? What's a few biological impurities compared to fistfuls of refined chemicals?"

"I hate you!"

He laughed and leaped to the other bank, and Helena followed, slipped on the wet grass, and lay spread-eagled. Hugh gripped her hand and hauled her up, and when they walked on, their hands still held, warming each other.

"I never know when to take you seriously," Helena complained.

"Taking things seriously makes you depressed," said Hugh.

"That's your experience, is it?"

"Isn't it yours?"

"I don't have to live with your kind of poverty," said Helena.

"What's money got to do with it?"

"It has to make a difference," said Helena.

"Well I wouldn't know," said Hugh.

"You will soon," she told him.

"I'm still not sure it's the answer," he said.

"The answer to what?"

"Everybody's problems and the problems of the world. I mean if earning money is our only purpose in life, and spending it is our only pleasure . . . then what about the unemployed and the starving millions? What's their purpose? And where's their pleasure? And aren't we just perpetuating a system that doesn't work, that has always been unjust and is anyway falling apart? What we ought to be doing is finding some kind of alternative existence, a way of sharing what we have, and a lifestyle that doesn't diminish the world's natural resources."

"They were saying that fifty years ago," said Helena.

"But they didn't *do* anything," said Hugh.

"No," said Helena. "That's why we have power cuts . . . why we're using coal again instead of oil . . . why goods are

100

moved by rail instead of road transport . . . why there are almost no cars and imported foodstuffs are rationed. Everyone's affected, Hugh."

"And some more than others," said Hugh.

"Meaning me, I suppose?"

"If the cap fits . . ."

"Just because my father . . ."

He squeezed her hand. "You're taking things seriously again."

"Maybe we should change the subject?" Helena suggested.

"So what else is important?"

"Us?" said Helena.

■ ■ ■

They made a wide sweeping circuit of the hills and returned, late in the afternoon, to Highview House. There was a stile into a paddock, and a security gate between the cowshed and the house that gave access to the yard. Helena unlocked it, the great divide between the two of them, and automatically Hugh turned to go. But she invited him in for a sandwich.

"Or better still, why don't you stay for dinner and meet my father? I don't suppose Mommy will mind."

He regarded her uncertainly.

"I'm not exactly dressed for dinner," he said.

"That doesn't matter," said Helena. "It's Angharad's afternoon off anyway, so we shan't be having anything special. Do stay, Hugh."

Gravel scrunched beneath her boots, wedged in the holes in Hugh's sneakers as he limped behind her and made pale scratches on the utility-room floor. A freezer hummed, powered by bottled gas, and a washing machine waited beside it. There was a bathroom, with a shower and toilet, and a built-in closet containing spare footwear, a vacuum cleaner and a coat rack. But Hugh kept his parka on, conscious of the worn shirt beneath it.

The kitchen was huge, big as the whole ground floor of the terraced house in which they squatted, luxury such as Hugh had never seen before except in glossy magazines. A copper kettle sang on a scarlet stove, and copper saucepans shone on a shelf, and glass-fronted cabinets displayed bone china plates and cups and serving tureens, a set of scarlet casseroles and cordon-bleu cookbooks. Pale oak cupboards and marbled work surfaces surrounded the walls, and the oven mitts matched the curtains, and padded stools were arranged by the breakfast bar. Pots of scarlet geraniums bloomed on the windowsill.

He stood awkwardly, not knowing what else to do. He was out of place, afraid to tread on the polished wood floor, afraid to mar the shine of things by breath or touch or the shabbiness of his presence. But Helena appeared not to notice. She opened a can of salmon, mixed it with mayonnaise, made sandwiches and coffee.

"I'm afraid it's only instant," she said. "The coffeemaker got broken in the move and we haven't replaced it. And don't just stand there—grab a seat and make yourself at home. Do you take sugar?"

"No," said Hugh.

Helena placed a flowered mug before him.

Then her mother entered the kitchen, wearing a pink velvet dressing gown and pink fluffy slippers. Her hair was wet from recent washing . . . bleached blond with darkness at the roots.

102

"I thought I heard noises . . ."

"I'm just making a couple of sandwiches," said Helena.

"So I see," Mrs. Boyd said primly.

"And this is Hugh," said Helena. "I've invited him to dinner."

Mrs. Boyd looked at him disdainfully.

Then looked away.

"When you invite people to dinner, Helena, I would prefer a little notice."

"If it's inconvenient . . ." Hugh began.

"It's only one extra place!" said Helena.

"It's also Angharad's afternoon off!" said Mrs. Boyd.

"So we'll have sausage and baked beans," said Helena. "Hugh won't mind. And do you remember when Daddy used to go jogging?"

"What about it?" asked Mrs. Boyd.

"I was just wondering," said Helena. "I mean Hugh needs a pair of shoes, and if Daddy won't be using his sneakers anymore . . . ?"

"What size is he?"

"Ten," said Hugh.

"I'll look for them," Mrs. Boyd said coldly.

"And could you find him a shirt and trousers as well?"

Annoyance flashed in Mrs. Boyd's eyes. "I don't know where you've been, and what you've been doing, but I certainly don't want to see you at the meal table looking like that. You'd better have a shower and change your clothes. *Him* too."

"His name's Hugh," said Helena.

"You know where the towels are," said Mrs. Boyd.

She left, closing the door.

"Cow!" said Helena.

"Maybe I ought to go," said Hugh.

"Just don't take any notice of her," Helena told him.

"Always like this with your friends, is she?"

"I don't have any friends, not really."

"Surely you must have some?"

"The girls at school are only out to impress."

"You must be lonely then?"

"I was until today," said Helena.

■ ■ ■

It was a strange few hours . . . almost as if Hugh were changed from himself into someone else. Showered and dressed in Mr. Boyd's clothes . . . a maroon-and-blue track suit, white socks and sneakers . . . smelling of talc and after-shave . . . he played a part, behaved in ways he would not normally have behaved, correctly, formally, obeying the unspoken rules of the house. And Helena behaved differently too, aware of her mother's presence, no longer touching him or holding his hand.

He trailed in her wake through countless rooms, admiring the parquet floors and Chinese carpets, pictures on the walls, the polished antique furniture and the bowl of freesias on the dining-room table. Everything he saw was beautiful and impressive . . . fine, valuable things . . . but he could not imagine living there, spending each and every day in those surroundings. Somehow the house restricted his freedom, suppressed his natural responses, demanded a kind of reverence impossible to keep up.

He played Chinese solitaire with Helena in the drawing room. A coal fire burned in the hearth, and the sunlight was bright over the gardens beyond the patio doors. After a while he felt stifled, wanted to go out in the air, walk, run, move, shout, express what he was and release his energy. But Helena had changed into a sky blue dress and thin shoes. And a six-mile hike over the hills was more than enough exercise for one day, she said. Anyway it was evening and the day would be growing chill. Indoors by the fire was a good place to be. And no, she did not feel cut off from something.

Then her father came home.

Helena went to speak to him in the hallway and Hugh was introduced. They shook hands politely.

"Pleased to meet you," said Mr. Boyd.

"How do you do, Mr. Boyd," said Hugh.

"Did you have a good journey from Cardiff?"

"Reasonable," said Hugh.

"You didn't come alone, I hear."

"No," said Hugh.

"Five of you," said Mr. Boyd.

"Not counting Dilys and Glenda," said Hugh.

"I'm not sure I can accommodate five of you."

"I want Hugh to stay," said Helena.

"Well, we'll talk about it later," said Mr. Boyd.

It was all very proper, as was the dinner in the dining room . . . white wine, and fancy place settings, damask table napkins, crisp rolls and thin soup, and silver cutlery. But Hugh chose the wrong spoon.

"That one's for the dessert," said Helena.

"Does it matter?" asked Hugh.

"It matters to me," said Mrs. Boyd.

Mr. Boyd chuckled. "We have to uphold our pretensions, son. It's all we have left to cling to, the only thing that distinguishes us from the common people. If you question the use of a soup spoon, the last bastion between rich and poor might start to crumble. And then where would we be?"

105

"Equal in spite of our differences?" said Hugh.

"I don't think we're quite ready for that one."

"Has to come though, doesn't it?"

"But not in our lifetime, son."

Mrs. Boyd gathered up the empty dishes.

"There's fresh salmon mousse for the main course, with asparagus tips and duchess potatoes. I hope it's to everyone's taste."

"I'm sure it will be quite delicious," said Mr. Boyd.

"My friends'll be having sardine sandwiches," said Hugh.

Mrs. Boyd glared at him. "I don't need that kind of comparison, thank you very much!"

There was an awkward silence.

"In parts of Africa a sardine sandwich would probably feed five people for a week," said Mr. Boyd. "If we want to assuage our consciences, we shall have to raise our donation to the International Red Cross, I think."

"We give enough already!" Mrs. Boyd said crossly.

And she swept from the room.

"Have you ever considered joining the diplomatic service?" Mr. Boyd asked Hugh.

Helena giggled.

"Have some more wine," she said.

■   ■   ■

After the meringue cups filled with fruit and brandy, and coffee served with cream, Hugh accompanied Helena and her father across the yard to the barn that had been converted to a billiard room. There were benches along the walls and a bar at one end laden with drink. He learned how to handle a cue, and the game began . . . he and Helena

106

against Mr. Boyd, shadows around a table, colored balls speeding under the spotlights across green baize as the darkness deepened outside. And amid the fun and the laughter were snatches of a job interview . . . Hugh, the prospective employee, being questioned by the colliery manager.

"Why didn't you go on to higher education?"

"I couldn't afford to."

"There are student loans available."

"Afterward you have to pay it back," said Hugh.

"That's to be expected, of course."

"And if you can't get a job," said Hugh, "you're in debt for life. And what's the chances?"

"Considerably higher if you have a degree, I imagine."

"Yes," said Hugh. "There are several university graduates driving the Cardiff buses . . . a hundred and sixty ecu a week take-home pay, that's what they get. Not much, is it, for four years' study? They'll be lucky to pay off the interest, and never mind the loan itself. Higher education is only for the rich now, see?"

"Junior colleges are free," said Helena. "You can stay at a junior college until you're twenty-one. And then you can go on to various job-experience training programs."

"Which is one way of keeping down the unemployment figures," said Hugh. "And providing employers with a free source of labor."

"So you wouldn't be interested in job training?" asked Mr. Boyd. "Start next Tuesday, after the long weekend . . . a hundred ecu a week, which we'll claim direct from the welfare department, for you and your two young friends . . . with a guarantee of employment at the end of it. And full wages for the two men I interviewed this morning. It's the best I can offer if you want to stay together. Otherwise I can take you on but not the others, which is what was agreed in the first place."

"A hundred ecu a week is better than nothing," said Helena.

"Think about it," said Mr. Boyd.

Hugh thought.

But his head felt queer, the lights were too bright, and the billiard balls looked strange and blurred. And he could not make a decision anyway, not without asking the others, even though he already knew the answer. For Di's sake and David's sake they had to accept.

■ ■ ■

Helena closed the gates behind him.

"See you tomorrow."

"Yes," said Hugh.

And he waved his hand.

She watched him heading down the lane in the moonlight. His walk was unsteady, weaving from side to side as if he were drunk. Maybe he was, she thought, drunk from his own senses, just as she was. She felt high as a kite and tipsy with triumph. Hugh was hers . . . and the rest of her life would be like today, laughing and magical, always together. Her footsteps dancing, Helena returned to the house.

Her mother was in the drawing room, reading a magazine and watching the television news. The summit of world governments had banned the international trade in hardwoods in an attempt to preserve the remaining rain forests. A consequential rise in unemployment within subsidiaries of the building industry was to be expected.

"Where's Daddy?" asked Helena.

108

"In the barn playing billiards?" Mrs. Boyd suggested.

"The lights weren't on."

"Then I've no idea where he is."

Helena sat on the sofa beside her.

"I presume that boy has gone?" said Mrs. Boyd.

"I made sure the gates were locked," said Helena.

"He's left his clothes here."

"He'll be back tomorrow."

"I hope this is not going to become a regular thing."

"What if it does?"

"I'd rather he didn't come to this house, Helena."

"Why not?"

"Because he's not our kind, that's why!"

"I don't know what you mean," said Helena.

"He's totally lacking in refinement, for one thing."

"Daddy likes him!"

"There's no accounting for taste, of course."

"And I like him too!"

"He's not exactly suitable though, is he?"

"You're just a snob!" said Helena.

"And *you* have to concentrate on passing your exams."

"What's that got to do with Hugh?"

"You could do without the distraction, that's all."

"It's only for a couple of weeks," said Helena.

"Well, I'm not having him here!" said Mrs. Boyd.

"You can't stop me seeing him!"

"If you want to mess up your life, that's your affair."

"I hate you!" said Helena.

"Trouble?" asked Mr. Boyd from the doorway.

"Ask *her*!" said Helena. "I'm going to bed!"

She pushed past him, went running up the stairs to her room and slammed the door. It had been beautiful, wonderful, and now it was ruined . . . Hugh banned from the house, and she not allowed to invite him there. And where else could they go? Out on the hills, all day and every day in all kinds of weather? Damp grass and sheep shit? No warmth, no shelter and no conveniences? Maybe Hugh would accept it, but Helena could not. She had never really been an outdoor type. They would have to find somewhere, she thought. Somewhere they could go and be together. His place perhaps?

■ ■ ■

The kitchen was in darkness. Hugh groped his way in and failed to find the light switch. But the moon through the window showed him the exit. Alternately shivering and sweating in Mr. Boyd's track suit, he headed along the hallway to the front room, opened the door and clung to the wall to steady himself, blinking in the sudden light.

The contrast struck him.

He had walked on Chinese carpets costing thousands of ecu, eaten with silver spoons from bone china dishes, drunk fine wine and lived in luxury for a whole evening. But here was his real life . . . a room with bare floorboards and no furniture . . . cracked plates and stained mugs, and a gorse fire burning in the grate . . . smells of soot and smoke and Colin's socks . . . and they not knowing any other way, nor even dreaming of it.

They sat cross-legged on the floor, except for Glenda, who leaned against the wall. He noticed the scruffiness of their clothes and how unkempt they were. And there was a weariness in their faces that turned toward him, a dull acceptance in their eyes. They had given up hope, he thought, assumed

110

they were going home to Cardiff, catching the bus in the morning. Packed suitcases stood ready in the corner.

"Guess what," said Hugh.

"Humpty Dumpty was pushed?" said Di.

"You've taken up long-distance running?" said Glenda.

"Maroon and blue," said Flutey. "Now there's pretty."

"Clashes with the eyes though," said Colin.

"Bloodshot," said Flutey.

"You're sloshed!" said Dilys.

"Only slightly," said Hugh.

"Been hobnobbing with *her*, have you?"

"It was worth it, see?"

"So why don't you tell us?" said Colin.

"We start work next Tuesday," said Hugh.

The room turned wild.

Suddenly they were all on their feet, laughing, cheering, hugging each other, capering about. With tears in her eyes, Glenda kissed David, kissed Hugh, and Di shook his hand, clapped him on the shoulder. Colin grinned, and Dilys and Flutey whirled and twisted in a crazy dance. And the room spun slowly beneath the light, red-flocked wallpaper revolving with a chaos of voices.

"We've done it!"

"We've got a job!"

"A real job!"

"Isn't it wonderful?"

"Let's celebrate, shall we?"

"Let's have a party tomorrow."

"I'll have to go back to Cardiff tomorrow," said Di. "Fetch the wife and kids, see?"

"Then we'll celebrate tonight."

"The pubs are still open."

"We'll go and buy a flagon of beer."

"Or a couple of bottles of cider?"

"There's a catch!" shouted Hugh.

Everything stopped.

And all eyes turned to him.

"A catch?" said David.

"What catch?" asked Di.

"Nothing to do with you," said Hugh. "You and David get full wages . . . but Colin, Flutey and I are on job training for the first twelve months. It was the best Mr. Boyd could offer . . . a hundred ecu a week . . . with a guaranteed job at the end of it."

"And you accepted?" asked Colin.

"No," said Hugh. "I said we'd let him know in the morning."

"Well, it's better than nothing," said Dilys.

"More than we'd ever get in Cardiff," said Flutey.

"Three hundred a week between four of us," said Dilys.

Colin shrugged. "We've got no choice, I suppose."

"That's what I thought," said Hugh.

"So we've got to accept it, don't we?"

"And we'll celebrate anyway," said Glenda.

"But the drinks are on us," said David.

"Who wants beer and who wants cider?" asked Di.

"And we saved you a sardine sandwich," Glenda told Hugh.

His stomach churned. Consommé and salmon mousse . . . meringue with brandy, white wine . . . he could not take any more. The very mention of cider and sardine sandwiches made him feel sick. The room spun in giddy circles, and cold sweat beaded his forehead, and his knees felt like jelly.

112

He sank, slowly, down the wall, landed on the floor with a hard thump.

They gathered around him.

"Hugh?"

"What's the matter, Hugh?"

"I feel terrible," he groaned.

"I told you he was sloshed," said Dilys.

9

Hugh did not come to Highview House the next morning. All day Helena waited for the gate bell to ring, but no one came . . . only her father returning from work in the evening, conveying apologies. The others had come into the colliery to accept the jobs that had been offered and collect instructions, but Hugh was ill apparently. Too much rich food, David had said, or maybe too much alcohol. He was ill the next day as well, or so Helena assumed, when once again he failed to arrive. And how long did it take, she wondered, to recover from a bilious attack or a hangover?

Saturday, too, passed with the sun bright over the hills as Helena fumed and fretted. He came in the evening, looking pale and tired. They had had to fix up some furniture and organize the sleeping arrangements, he said. And *they* obviously mattered more than she did, Helena thought bitterly. She did not invite him in. She was waiting for a phone call from a friend in Kent, she told him, and tomorrow she was going on a family outing to Carmarthen Castle.

"I left my clothes here," said Hugh.

"Is that the only reason you came?"

"No," said Hugh. "But if it happens to rain, I don't have another parka, see?"

Helena went to fetch them . . . and an old tweed jacket that her father no longer wore. And seeing him in the shadows of the beech trees waiting for her to return, she almost relented, almost forgot she was annoyed with him.

"What about Monday?" he asked her.

"What about it?" she said.

"See you then, will I?"

"Do you want to?" she asked him.

"Don't you know that?" he said.

"My mother doesn't approve of you," Helena informed him.

"I'm not interested in your mother," he said.

After that, Easter eggs meant nothing. Helena saved the best of them for him. And the trip to Carmarthen became a form of self-punishment, sunlit hours spent with her parents that she might have spent with Hugh. Her stupidity galled her.

And when Monday arrived, the hills were sodden from overnight rain. The sky stayed cloudy and the previous magic had gone. There was nowhere to sit, nowhere to linger, and Hugh seemed quiet and remote, his mind on other things and not on her. A cold wind whistled around the crags under which they sheltered.

"We could go to your place," said Helena.

"We're squatting," said Hugh.

115

"What difference does that make?"

"We're not supposed to be there, see?"

"But we can go there anyway, can't we?"

"Things are a bit difficult at the moment," said Hugh.

"You mean the others wouldn't want me there?"

"That's not it," said Hugh.

"So why can't we go there?" asked Helena.

He tried to explain. Compared to Highview House, Number Twenty-seven Bethesda Street was a hovel. There were no home comforts, no privacy, no hospitality he could offer her . . . just bare floorboards, trouble with the neighbors, and a lot of hostility and nastiness . . . and he really ought to be getting back in case something had happened. It was not fair to leave the others to cope with everything.

Helena felt peeved. She did not see why the others could not take care of themselves, or why Hugh felt he had to be there. And the fact that Glenda was pregnant had nothing to do with him. If there was trouble, she had her husband to protect her, as well as Flutey and Colin and Dilys. Or was it Dilys he wanted to go home for?

He denied it, of course, but he went home anyway . . . left Helena at the gates of Highview House without even a backward glance. It was as if their relationship no longer mattered, as if he had gained from her everything he could . . . jobs for his friends, and the means to survive, and her father's clothes . . . and an Easter egg filled with chocolates that her mother had given to her. She hoped he would choke on it, and his ingratitude filled her with fury.

Then he started work . . . the afternoon shift, from two o'clock until ten in the evening . . . and Helena did not see him again until the following Sunday. He arrived without warning and rang the gate bell. He had brought a picnic

116

from the corner shop . . . sandwiches and apples and two bags of potato chips . . . and he expected her to spend the day with him, as if nothing had happened. And nothing *had* to his way of thinking. If she was not important to him, he would not have come there, he said.

Then the hills were no longer timeless. The hours they spent together passed swiftly as minutes, until the sun set over Ynysceiber in a sky of fire. They parted at the gate among owl hoots and frost fall, with the chill stars over them and slate roofs shining in the valley. It was something to remember, two days later, when Helena returned to Kent.

■ ■ ■

It was not easy living in Ynysceiber. The local people resented them, and they had no right to be living where they did. The neighbors complained. The house belonged to old Mostyn Watkins who had died last year, and had passed to his sister, who was living with her daughter in Pontypridd. It was family property and up for sale . . . not a flophouse for vagrants. And Di and Mrs. Di had the same problem. They and their children, William and Olwen, had taken possession of an empty house opposite that belonged to Alun Morgan, who had emigrated to Australia. Lawyers' letters threatened court action . . . and the sheriff's office threatened with eviction. It was a ridiculous situation. People, in general, were leaving the valley, not seeking to live there, and there were dozens of vacant properties that would never be sold. But there was no such thing as squatters' rights in Ynysceiber. Nor was there any public housing or bed-and-breakfast accommodation available . . . not for outsiders.

So they stayed where they were and they had no choice. Beds were of heather carted from the hills, with blankets thrown over them . . . tables made from window boards with fence posts for legs, chairs reinforced fruit boxes begged from the corner shop, or a plank in the sitting room balanced between two piles of bricks. They cooked on a camp stove bought from their first week's wages . . . and the handcart, minus its wheels, was converted to a cradle ready for Glenda's baby. Everything temporary and unstable, reflecting their lives.

The real estate agents applied for tenancy agreements, but it made no difference. People still resented them. And those who lived in the street waged a vendetta of unpleasantness. At night the drunks gathered outside, banged on the doors and shouted abuse. Dilys, Glenda and Mrs. Di were cold-shouldered by the local women . . . and Di and David, Colin, Flutey and Hugh were shunned in the Collier's Arms pub and down the mine . . . Flutey in particular, the only black person in Ynysceiber, gaining job experience when local unemployed youths could not. Somebody wrote "Fuck off, Coon" in crayon on the front-room window.

Dilys fumed.

Mrs. Di worried.

William and Olwen were bullied at school.

Flutey was afraid to leave the house unaccompanied.

Glenda grew more and more weepy.

And David fretted about finding a place of their own.

"You don't have to," said Dilys.

"Best if we stay together anyway," said Colin.

"It's not safe for Glenda to be by herself," said Flutey. "Anything could happen while you're away at work."

"But what about the baby?" asked David.

"We're willing to accept it," said Colin.

"It'll be part of the family anyway," said Flutey.

"And I like babies," said Dilys.

Hugh was too exhausted even to express an opinion. His muscles ached from hacking coal all day . . . his body clock had gone haywire due to the changing shifts . . . and there were letters from his mother and Helena he had no time to answer. It was not the work itself Hugh found difficult; it was the deprivation . . . the loss of days and nights, sunlight and moonlight, the world and its seasons . . . the whole meaning of his life being eroded. He began to dread the winding wheel turning and the slow daily descent into the underground darkness.

It was not totally dark. A generator above ground supplied a feeble light to the naked electric bulbs that were strung along the main tunnel. But in the side shafts, where they cut the coal from the living rock, there were only the frail gleams of light from their helmets. Metal pit props held up the roof, and Welsh voices echoed amid the rattle of shovels and the hacking of picks. Trams clattered, were hauled to the surface and returned empty in a never-ending succession.

They worked eight hours a day, six days a week, in a space too low to stand up in . . . bending, kneeling, lying, in a seepage of water and a miasma of coal dust . . . black up their noses, in their clothes, in the pores of their skin. And the coal they cut loose fell onto a conveyor belt, where a miner at the far end shoveled it into the nearest tram.

They were allowed half an hour for lunch, time to stretch their legs in the main tunnel, piss against a rock wall and eat the sandwiches Dilys had made . . . a break that was no break at all from the infernal cold and the infernal darkness. And when, at the end of the shift, Hugh entered the cage that carried him to the surface, he was too worn out to make use of what remained of the day or night . . . he just wanted to fall into bed and sleep.

"You'll get used to it," said Colin.

"We all will," said Flutey.

"It's bound to take us a while to adapt."

"By the time we've been here six months . . ."

"It'll be winter," said Hugh. "We're missing out on everything, see? That's what I find hard to accept. It's like the world doesn't exist anymore, not for us."

"It would be the same whatever job we had," said Colin.

"And only another forty-five years before we retire," said Flutey.

Hugh sighed. "That's what it's all about, is it? That's the purpose of human existence?"

It was the miner on the shovel who answered him.

"Speed it up, you lot! You're not here to enjoy yourselves, you're here to work! No time for yakking, there is! I got my production bonus to think of, see?"

Hugh brushed the coal dust from his eyes.

This was not job experience.

This was a life sentence.

And his only crime was being born.

And Helena was a girl he now and then wrote to, belonging to another world, another time, so long ago he could hardly remember. Mostly he was absent even from his own memories, down the pit in a dark reality that erased all else. For a hundred ecu a week Hugh had sold himself.

■ ■ ■

For Helena, memories were important. She relived them constantly . . . Hugh in her mind through every waking

120

moment, during lessons or reviewing for exams. She wrote him letters and waited for his replies . . . hated him when they failed to arrive, and loved him when he did finally write to her. He was all she cared about. Irrelevant the study of European political history, sociology and economics, Shakespeare or the Nun's Priest's Tale . . . nothing to do with the meaning of her life. She failed to concentrate on anything, and during the examinations her head became a blank.

Then it was over . . . her childhood . . . her schooling . . . her years in Kent. She returned, thankfully, to Wales . . . to summer in the valley, and long carefree weeks between past and future that she thought she would spend with Hugh. For the first time in her life she felt free . . . released from studying, released from any other obligation, not knowing or caring what would become of her until her examination results arrived at the end of August.

At first she did nothing, just relaxed on the sunbed on the patio, rubbed her skin with lotion and gained a rich gold tan. Above her the hills were cracked and dried, and massed flowers wilted in the garden, and sprinklers kept the lawns alive. A part-time gardener, hired for the summer, raked and weeded and ogled her. She was exhibiting herself, her mother said curtly, lounging about seminaked in front of that man! And she could hardly expect her father to keep her in idleness for the rest of her life, so it was about time she made herself useful!

Reluctantly Helena shelled peas and hulled strawberries, dusted her bedroom and waited for Hugh to visit. Days passed, long and slow and boring, and he did not come . . . and her father kept forgetting to check which shift he was on. Maybe he had not received her last letter? Helena thought. Maybe he had not yet realized she was home? Or maybe he had found someone else? Dilys perhaps?

That night she lay awake wondering. And the next afternoon she went to find him, headed down the lane into town. She stopped at the corner shop and asked directions. She was almost there, the shopkeeper told her. Bethesda Street was around the corner. But there were groups of women gossiping on the sidewalk, heads that turned and eyes that watched her. And she heard their whispering mingled with the sound of the river below.

"That's Mr. Boyd's daughter, isn't it?"

"Angharad said she was home."

"Looks like her mother, doesn't she?"

"Another Lady Muck."

"Lovely sandals she's wearing."

"And a lovely sundress too."

"Bet she didn't get that from the secondhand shop."

"And what's she doing here then?"

"Visiting, is it?"

"Deigning to grace us with her presence?"

It was too late to turn back, too late to wish she had not come. Helena rounded the corner of the end terrace. A girl with freckles and red hair sat on an upturned box sewing a patch on a pair of jeans. And a pregnant woman made baby clothes from a piece of old sheeting. Two pairs of eyes, soft hazel and fierce blue, stared at Helena.

"Does Hugh Davies live here?" she asked nervously.

"Who wants to know?" asked the girl.

"Are you Helena?" asked the woman.

"Yes," said Helena.

"I'm Glenda," said the woman. "And this is Dilys. Hugh's at work, I'm afraid. He won't be home until late."

"But we'll tell him you called," said Dilys.

She was being dismissed . . . not wanted there, not welcome, no more than Hugh was welcome at Highview House. She did not need to ask why. The answer was obvious. Dilys had something going for Hugh. She could see it in her eyes and in her smile. She had come there from Cardiff, lived in the same house with him, and she was attractive too. Bitter feelings twisted inside Helena and she turned to go . . . but the women had followed her, a group of them standing on the edge of the empty lot.

Their voices were venomous.

"I see!"

"That's the way the wind blows, is it?"

"Lining up a few more jobs for your friends, are we?"

"Hobnobbing with the management!"

"Smarming your way in!"

"Fuck off!" Dilys told them.

But the women advanced.

Their attention turned on Helena.

"And what about us, Miss High-and-Mighty?"

"Jobs for the whole valley your father promised."

"Another pit opening in Ynysceiber."

"Next year we were told."

"But he hasn't delivered, has he?"

"Our men are still waiting."

"And those who are working are working for a pittance!"

Helena backed toward the gate.

"Fuck off! All of you!" Dilys repeated angrily.

And Glenda struggled to her feet. "You'd better come in, Helena."

"That's going to make things worse!" said Dilys.

"Are we going to behave like our neighbors?" asked

123

Glenda. She opened the gate. "Come inside until they've gone," she told Helena. "And you go and put the kettle on," she said to Dilys.

It was an uneasy sanctuary. Helena hated it . . . a ramshackle kitchen with nothing in it but a makeshift table and a camp stove. Tea bags were hung to dry on a line above the sink, and a fly buzzed against the window. They waited in silence, and outside the women went on shouting. David, who was working the night shift and had been sleeping upstairs, came blinking into the sunlight. He was wearing nothing but sandals and a pair of underpants. Helena flushed with embarrassment.

"Trouble?" he asked.

"Stupid cows!" Dilys said angrily.

"This is Helena," said Glenda. "Hugh's Helena."

Dilys sniffed.

"Ah," said David. "*Bore da*, Miss Helena. You the cause of all the noise, are you?"

His words accused, although he smiled at her, and Helena felt even more awkward. Outside the shouting increased. New voices were added. Then, a moment later, a bald-headed man and a skinny middle-aged woman with graying hair appeared in the doorway.

"You all right, Glenda *bach*?"

"You ought to be resting, not on your feet making tea."

"She's not," Dilys said sourly. "I'm making it."

"Who's the young lady?"

"Mr. Boyd's daughter," said David.

"Helena," said Glenda.

"Ah," said the man. "So that's who they were carrying on about." He held out his hand. "I'm Di and this is Mrs.

Di. Nice to meet you, Miss Helena. A pity Hugh's not here . . . but with the boys away it gives the men a chance."

Dilys sniffed again.

Mrs. Di laughed.

And Di's blue eyes twinkled kindly.

"Old carrottop giving you a hard time, is she? A touch of the pea-green monster it is, see? She is setting her cap at our Hugh, but he is blind to everyone except you."

"You rotten bastard!" said Dilys. "It's not like that at all!" She offered Helena a brown paper bag containing broken cookies. "Take no notice of him," she said. "And don't take all the custard creams . . . they're mine."

Suddenly Helena smiled.

Slowly, as the afternoon passed, she got to know them.

And she began to see why these people mattered to Hugh.

They were mad, crazy, Welsh as the hills. She loved the lilt of their voices, their teasing and bantering, their warm interactions and their affection for each other. She loved what they were . . . Glenda, hugely pregnant and glad of it . . . Mrs. Di, the prospective midwife, garrulous and motherly . . . David, courteous and concerned. She even liked Dilys, admired her spirit and her uncompromising honesty. And later Di's children, William and Olwen, arrived home from school . . . the girl from the station cafeteria, thin faced and scrawny with a gap-toothed grin, recognizing Helena, who recognized her.

"I gave Hugh your message," she said.

"I heard you did," said Helena.

"Broadcast it everywhere," said Glenda.

"Not exactly discreet is our Olwen," said David.

"A mouth worse than Dilys," said Di.

"One day, baldy, I'm going to fill yours in!" said Dilys.

They sat on boxes in the yard. And what had seemed to Helena to be some kind of party was just part of their everyday lives. It was nothing unusual, said Dilys, just friends being together, having a laugh and a chat. No point in standing on ceremony, was there?

No, thought Helena.

And their parting words echoed in her head.

"Come and visit us again."

"Whenever you like, see?"

"Always welcome, you are."

"And Hugh's on mornings next week."

"So we'll be expecting you."

They meant it, thought Helena.

They really meant it.

And it had nothing to do with being her father's daughter.

■ ■ ■

Di accompanied Helena up the lane to ensure she got home safely. And the unfriendliness of Highview House seemed sad and horrible, full of silence and meaningless things and her mother's disapproval. Socializing with colliery employees was hardly desirable, said Mrs. Boyd. They had a position to maintain, and it could make things very awkward for her father. And whether or not the miners were paid fair wages was none of Helena's concern, nor Mrs. Boyd's either.

"Some local women were complaining," said Helena.

"That's exactly what I mean!" said Mrs. Boyd.

"But if they're not getting enough . . ."

"Wages have to be linked to company profits, Helena."

"We don't go short, though, do we?"

"Your father is the colliery manager, for goodness' sake."

"So as long as the management and the directors are all right, it doesn't matter if the workers are being exploited?"

"Don't be so melodramatic!" said Mrs. Boyd.

"Maybe I ought to have a word with Daddy."

"Who put you up to this?"

"No one!"

"That damned boy, I suppose?"

"Hugh wasn't there!"

"He ought to be grateful he's got a job at all!" said Mrs. Boyd. "And you need to remember which side your bread is buttered on, Helena! Without the British Mining Company you'd have precious little to write home about. And you haven't, by any chance, seen your father's old tweed jacket recently?"

"No," lied Helena.

"I suppose Angharad must have taken it," said Mrs. Boyd. "You can't trust these domestics nowadays."

Helena went to her room.

Everything her mother said seemed somehow hateful.

And true richness had nothing to do with money . . . it was a terraced house with nothing in it, a backyard and sunlight, cracked mugs, broken cookies, and people who liked each other and liked her. Hugh was lucky, she thought, to be living with them.

And, in spite of her mother, she went there again . . . many times . . . until almost she felt she was one of them.

10

An hour before midnight Glenda went into labor, although Hugh slept unaware until Dilys woke him. Colin ran to the mine to fetch David from the night shift, and Flutey fetched Mrs. Di from across the street, stayed there to mind her children. But Hugh remained, brewed raspberry-leaf tea to ease Glenda's pain, and listened to the silences that interspersed her cries, the agony of birthing no one of the male sex could ever really know. Yet the experience touched him. It was almost as if Glenda were his wife and the coming child his own. If she died in the process, he knew he would grieve for the loss of her almost as much as David. Four months of sharing each other's lives had inextricably bound them together.

Bound them all, thought Hugh.

And how could Helena fit into that?

Her return to Ynisceiber had disturbed him. Often, when

he came home from the colliery, he found her waiting . . . sitting on an upturned box in the yard chattering with Glenda and Dilys. It was better than being at home with her mother, she said. Yet she did not belong here. She belonged to a world of ease and luxury, everything money could buy. It was one thing to visit and enjoy their company, but he could hardly expect her to relinquish everything she had to share his life. Nor could he ever hope to keep her in the style to which she was accustomed. In reality he and Helena had no future together. And he ought to tell her, he thought. He ought to break with her before their relationship turned serious.

On the camp stove the kettle simmered.

And upstairs Glenda groaned.

Then Dilys came into the kitchen.

And Hugh forgot Helena and leaped to his feet.

"Want me to go for a doctor, do you?"

"No," said Dilys, "she's doing fine."

"More raspberry-leaf tea, is it?"

"Ordinary tea," said Dilys. "For me and Mrs. Di."

Hugh unpegged the tea bags, dropped them in the pot, refilled the kettle, and set it to boil again.

"How long's she going to be?" he asked.

"However long it takes," said Dilys. "All night and all tomorrow, if necessary."

"Oh God," said Hugh. "I'll never stand it."

Dilys grinned. "According to Mam . . . if women had the first child and men had the second, there would never be a third."

"Doesn't it scare you?" asked Hugh.

"Mrs. Di says that once it's over, you forget about the pain."

129

"I don't understand how any woman can volunteer to undergo that kind of agony," said Hugh.

"It's an instinct," said Dilys. "And why does it have to be painful anyway? In Africa women squat at the side of the fields and go on with their work five minutes later. It ought to be like that for us too. Maybe it will, once we stop expecting it to be difficult. At least most women have their babies at home now, instead of in hospitals like they used to. That's got to be a move in the right direction."

It was an odd conversation to be having in the middle of the night, strange and intimate, as if something had opened up between them, a channel of honesty such as Hugh had not dreamed could exist with a girl. And now, it seemed, there was nothing he could not discuss with Dilys, however deep, however personal.

"I can't imagine Helena squatting at the side of a field."

"No," said Dilys.

"She'd book into a private clinic, I suppose?"

"At a thousand ecu a day," said Dilys.

Hugh poured tea.

And Dilys watched him.

Light shone like fire on her wild red hair.

"It'll never work," she said quietly.

"What won't?" he asked her.

"You and Helena," she said.

"No," said Hugh.

"I mean I've got nothing against her," said Dilys. "I quite like her, see? Much better than I thought I would. And I know how much we owe her. But it stands to reason, doesn't it?"

"That's what I thought," said Hugh.

"Then you're going to have to tell her, aren't you?"

Hugh sighed.

"I wish there was some other way."

"Well, there isn't," Dilys said brutally. "And better to tell her sooner rather than later. Better for her, see?"

She took the tea and returned upstairs.

And Hugh had the rest of the night to sit and think . . . the rest of the night with Glenda upstairs, and the pain of her body going on and on . . . David returning to be there with her, and Colin dozing on the makeshift sofa that was usually Dilys's bed . . . the rest of the night with the interconnectedness of love, and life, and death, running through his head.

Then in the new day a new life began.

"Listen!" said Colin.

Upstairs they heard the child cry . . . and the summer dawn was pink across the valley. A girl, said Dilys, and they were calling her Rhiannon. Hugh saw her later before he went to work. She was small and wrinkled in her mother's arms, tiny fingers curling around his own. He saw the shine of Glenda's eyes and David's pride, and was glad for them both. And the pain of childbirth was soon forgotten, Dilys had said. But not the pain Helena would feel because of Hugh.

■　■　■

Light gleams winked on the black surface of the coal seam, fled to darkness again as the pickaxe struck . . . winked and fled, winked and fled . . . minuscule moments of rainbow beauty Hugh had to destroy. Hack . . . smash . . . coal dust was gritty in his mouth and time muddled in his head.

Was it only that morning Rhiannon had been born? Only yesterday he and Helena had been together? He remembered the sun on her hair and her blue laughing eyes, her touch, her kiss. They had walked for hours . . . over the hills, along the sheep paths and through the heather. It was the only time he felt truly alive . . . when he was out on the hills with her . . . the only time he felt clean and free.

Hack-smash . . . loose coal rattled onto the conveyor belt and was carried away. And only forty-five years to go before he retired, Flutey had said, forty-five years of selling himself for a bare existence. It would be the same whatever job he was in. Differentials eroded across the board in an attempt to maintain a degree of mass employment. No matter how hard Hugh worked, he would never have anything to offer a girl like Helena. And sooner or later he would have to tell her. This afternoon maybe?

"You're quiet," said Flutey.

"Positively melancholic," said Colin.

"Some of us didn't get any sleep last night," said Hugh.

And sleeplessness played tricks with his eyes. He saw someone smiling at him from the darkness of the tunnel. The miner squatted on his haunches.

"A word with you, brothers?"

"What about?" said Hugh.

"We are convening a union meeting, after the shift in the pit-head baths, which I am inviting you to attend."

"I didn't know there was a union," said Hugh.

"There isn't," said Colin.

"But there will be," said the miner. "And it is in your own best interests to belong to it, see? We are needing to redress the balance, brothers, between those who work for a living and those who are unemployed. The income of a miner, in many cases, is almost identical to the level of welfare benefits . . . and that is a blatant injustice. We are

132

intending to be putting our case to the management in the strongest possible terms. And if our demands are not met, we shall be withdrawing our labor. The right to strike is about to be reinstated in the annals of British industry. One out, all out . . . that's how it used to be and that's what it will be again. We shall be counting on you, brothers. When we are raising our hands in agreement, yours will be among them. Right?"

"You mean it's obligatory?" asked Hugh.

"We shall be honoring the choice of the individual, of course. It is every man's right to act according to his conscience. That is the basis of the democratic system. Everyone is free to vote against the motion as they see fit. But I wouldn't advise it. In a mining community there is no place for scabs, see?"

"I've already found that out," muttered Flutey.

"We all have," said Colin.

"We're the Cardiff colony of pariahs," said Hugh.

"If you ass-kiss your way in here, what do you expect?" asked the miner. "But in return for our overlooking that particular bone of contention, the least you can do is support us, see?"

"We'll give it our due consideration," said Hugh. "Henceforth and notwithstanding . . . and not forgetting the common consensus of opinion which will be heretofore diversely agreed upon."

There was a heavy silence.

The hacking of picks echoed in the distance.

And far away the trams rattled.

"I see," said the miner.

He backed down the tunnel on his hands and knees.

"You shouldn't have said that!" muttered Colin.

"Why not?" asked Hugh.

"If we don't go along with them, we're never going to be accepted."

"And you've probably made things worse," said Flutey.

In Hugh something snapped. He aimed the pickaxe. Several almighty blows smashed at the coal seam that split and crumbled and came crashing down, spilled from the conveyor belt onto the floor of the shaft in which they were working. But his voice was louder than the noise.

"For Christ's sake, who wants to be accepted in a place like Ynysceiber? And what can be worse than what we're doing now? This isn't living . . . it's bloody purgatory!"

■ ■ ■

"Isn't she beautiful?" said Dilys.

Helena gazed at the baby asleep in the crib. It was pink and wizened, with a shock of jet-black hair, not beautiful at all to her. But she would buy it something, she thought. She would like to do that. Carved wooden runners rattled on the flagstones of the yard as Dilys rocked it.

"Don't you like babies?"

Helena shrugged. "I've never had anything to do with them."

"I was thirteen when Mam had our Jimmy," said Dilys. "It was like sharing him, see? And I'll be sharing Rhiannon with Glenda as long as she stays. So if I never have any children of my own, it won't matter too much."

"That's one way of solving the overpopulation problem," said Helena.

Dilys grinned. "Shall I put the kettle on?"

"How long's Hugh going to be?" asked Helena.

"He should have been here half an hour ago," said Dilys.

134

A meal of bread and cheese and salad waited on the make-shift table, and tea brewed in the pot when Hugh and Colin and Flutey finally returned. They had stayed for a union meeting, they said, and there was talk of a strike over wages.

Helena sat on the doorstep. "Wages have to be linked to company profits," she said.

"Try telling that to the miners," said Colin.

"Di only brings home about twenty-five ecu a week more than when he was unemployed," said Flutey. "Which is hardly worth working for."

"And he's not the only one," said Colin.

"Daddy doesn't decide what the wage will be," said Helena.

"He's the colliery manager, isn't he?"

"He's also an employee like everyone else."

"And how will we manage if there's a strike?" asked Dilys. "How will we pay the electric bill and pay for food? Have they even thought of that?"

"If there *is* a strike," said Helena, "Sir Gerald Fraser is likely to have a fit. And he'll never open that second coal mine."

"More money's not the answer anyway," said Hugh.

"What do you mean?" asked Colin.

"Nothing can compensate for giving up your life in servitude, can it?"

Helena stared at him.

"Is that really how you see it?"

"He's just tired from lack of sleep last night," Dilys explained.

Hugh *was* tired. Helena could see it in the shadows beneath his eyes, sense it in his silence and in the drag of his footsteps as they went down the street. There was a market every two weeks in the parking lot by the river, stands selling handicrafts and battered vans come up from Cardiff. She wanted to go there to buy a present for the baby, and automatically Hugh accompanied her. But maybe he did not want to?

"I can go on my own," she said.

"It's not safe," he told her.

She understood why. She was recognized now in Ynysceiber. In the crowded market heads turned and eyes watched her, hated her, envied her for who she was, and where she lived, and all she possessed. People whispered, nudged each other, nodded toward her. And she clung to Hugh's arm, as if by displaying their relationship she made herself one with him, no different from anyone else. He helped her forget her position and her parentage, and kept the malice at bay. And the bright goods distracted her . . . fake silks shot with sunlight, embroidered slippers, gaudy clothes, and imported household items . . . everything cheap and shoddy and not worth buying.

But the crafts stands were better . . . homemade cakes and pastries, baskets of fruit and vegetables from gardens, hand-knitted sweaters, pine stools and pottery. She fingered a pink layette, its lacy dress and bonnet and booties all made to match.

"Do you think Glenda would like it?"

"It's ninety-five ecu!" said Hugh.

"That's not what I asked," said Helena.

She bought it anyway.

And two ice-cream cones from a refrigerated van.

They leaned on the wall to eat them. Sunlight was warm on their backs, and the river was dark and brown beneath them, streaming between stones and spoiled by the rubbish of ages, rusting cans and plastic bags and bits of discarded bicycles.

"You meant what you said, didn't you?"

"Meant what?" asked Hugh.

"About the job," said Helena.

"I've not got the right attitude, see?"

"It can't be very nice anyway," said Helena.

"I could think of better ways of spending my time," Hugh admitted.

"Maybe if I talked to Daddy, he could find you a job in the office?"

"You can't keep asking your father for favors on my behalf!"

"But if you really don't like being a miner . . ."

"That's not what I meant," said Hugh.

His voice was sharp, almost hostile, and his eyes were brooding on the river, not looking at her. And sounds of the market were loud and raucous behind her, but all Helena heard was a silence she did not understand.

"Hugh?"

"There's something I've got to tell you, Helena."

She waited.

And a sudden dread grew inside her.

"You and me . . ." said Hugh.

"What about us?" Helena asked fearfully.

He put his arm around her shoulders. "I care, see?"

She felt the relief, rested her head fondly against him. "I care about you too."

"But it won't work," said Hugh.

She stayed where she was, still, motionless.

She knew what he meant, but she did not want to know.

"We've got to stop seeing each other, *cariad*."

137

His voice tore at her.

And the reaction happened.

She turned to face him.

"You can't do that, Hugh!"

"It's not that I am wanting to."

"Then why are you?"

"Your world and mine . . . they just don't mix, girlie."

"I don't understand what you're saying!"

His eyes were gray and unflinching, fixed on her own.

"Think about it," he said. "I can't be dragging you down to where I am, Helena, not if I care. It is give and take in a relationship, see? And you are giving and I am taking and I have nothing of my own to give to you and never will have. Your mother is right not to approve of me. She is knowing full well we can have no future together."

"Don't say that, Hugh!"

Tears trickled down her face.

And he touched them gently.

"I'm sorry," he said. "But you've got to think about what you want from life, see?"

"I want *you*," she said brokenly.

He shook his head. "Talk about it again, shall we? Some other time?"

"I'd rather not talk about it at all," said Helena.

"No, all right then."

He kissed her gently.

And when she looked around everyone was watching.

■　■　■

They returned to the terraced house as if nothing had happened. And Glenda was up already, sitting in the sunlit yard nursing her baby . . . David beside her and Colin opposite

138

on an upturned bucket. Her breast was pale and exposed, and just for a moment Helena felt embarrassed, but no one else seemed to notice. Flutey brought her a glass of water, and Hugh simply smiled and touched her shoulder, lovingly, as he passed. He fetched boxes from the house for himself and Helena to sit on. Later Di and Mrs. Di, William and Olwen came to admire the baby and the new pink layette. And the party was complete, except for Dilys, who had fallen asleep in the front room.

But inside Helena was a new and terrible awareness. She was playing a part and all the time she feared it would not last. And it was not just Hugh she might be losing but the others as well. They were all part of her life now, and she could not imagine being without them. She remembered how it was in Penarth . . . days and weeks with no one to talk with, no one to laugh with, no one to care. She did not want to live like that again. She was afraid of being friendless and lonely. And not even Hugh could take the fear away. His hand held hers going back up the lane, but she felt no comfort.

"I didn't mean to upset you," he said.

"Then why did you?" she asked him.

"One of us has to be realistic, see?"

"And will I see you tomorrow?"

"If you want to," said Hugh.

"Meaning you'd rather not?"

"That's not the reason and you know it!"

She closed the gate.

"I don't think I know anything anymore," she replied.

She watched him head away up the track toward the silence of the hills. She wanted to run after him, beg him never to leave her, make him promise. But there were other ways of holding him. Evening shadows slanted through the beech trees and made speckles of gold on the gravel drive as she went toward the house. And Angharad rounded the corner, carrying a basket containing leftover food, leaving for home. She grinned, stupidly, at Helena.

"Had a nice afternoon, miss?"

"Yes thank you," Helena retorted.

And in the kitchen Helena's mother was waiting.

There was a pie on the counter.

And vegetables fresh from the market.

"I want a word with you," Mrs. Boyd said ominously.

"What about?" asked Helena.

"You and that boy! Kissing! In front of the whole town! Angharad saw you! Disgraceful behavior! I didn't bring you up to behave like that!"

"It wasn't like that anyway!" Helena told her.

"I don't know what your father will say when he hears about it!" Mrs. Boyd went on. "He'll be a laughingstock! His own daughter canoodling in public like a common slut!"

"It wasn't like that!" Helena shouted.

"Well, that's how it appeared!" said Mrs. Boyd.

"Appearances don't matter!"

"Of course they matter! People notice, Helena. Angharad noticed. Everyone noticed. I don't know how you can lower yourself to associate with that boy, let alone put on a display of physical intimacy!"

"What's wrong with it?" asked Helena. "It's natural, isn't it? He's male and I'm female. And what have you got against him?"

Mrs. Boyd stared at her.

And the harshness faded from her eyes.

"I've got nothing against him," she said. "Not personally.

140

I daresay he's decent enough in his way. It's you I'm thinking of, Helena. He's just not your kind, is he? He's got no background, no educational qualifications, no chance of getting on in life. What kind of future would you have with him? He has nothing to offer you . . . just some kind of sleazy existence that you can't even imagine. Think about it. And if you care about yourself at all, then put a stop to it."

The words cut, echoing Hugh's, reopening the wound.

But it was not Hugh being torn apart.

It was Helena.

And she could not bear her mother's pity.

"I'm sorry, dear, but it had to be said. It can't go on, can it? I think we'll go on vacation . . . a few weeks by the Mediterranean . . . rent a villa. It might help you forget."

"I don't want to forget!" Helena said bitterly. "And I don't want to go on vacation with you, either!"

"Do be sensible," begged Mrs. Boyd.

The fight went on, grew nastier and nastier. And if Helena wanted her university fees paid, it seemed, she would have to give in and go along with her mother. So all right, she decided. She would go on vacation . . . put some space and time between herself and Hugh. But it would not change what she felt. And before she went, she would talk to her father, have Hugh transferred from the coal face and advance his career. When he ended up as a colliery manager, then neither her mother nor Hugh himself could possibly object.

11

July became August. The valley sweltered and the river dried to a trickle. Hugh received postcards from the South of France, where Helena and her mother were staying. But Mr. Boyd remained on duty at the colliery, listening to the grievances of the miners and mediating with the company head office in London. Overtime payments were offered in exchange for voluntary layoffs, which were not forthcoming, but the directors flatly refused to negotiate an increased-wage settlement. It was inevitable then that the miners would call a strike. The order came in the middle of the afternoon shift. There was a mass walkout, and Di and David returned home.

"No one is to report for work again until we receive notice from the union," said David.

"So how will we manage?" asked Dilys.

"You'll have to sign up for welfare," said Glenda.

"Strikers don't qualify," said Di.

"And the union's not been going long enough to offer us strike payment," said David.

"You mean we'll have to manage on what little we've got saved?"

"I've got nothing saved," said Di.

"If we pool our resources, how long can we last?" asked Colin.

"I'm not going to take from you," said Di.

"How long?" repeated Colin.

"Three weeks at most," said Dilys.

"Unless we keep working," said Hugh. "If we go in each day, they have to pay us, don't they?"

The day's heat rebounded from the flagstones of the yard.

They could hear the cries of sheep on the hills.

And shouts of men in the street.

"If we do that," said David, "we won't be exactly popular, will we? We'll be scabs, see? In a closed community people won't take kindly to that. They're likely to turn nasty."

"And we've had enough nastiness already," said Flutey.

"There'll be pickets at the main gates anyway," said Colin. "They won't let us through."

"So we're going to allow ourselves to be intimidated, are we?" said Hugh.

Their voices assailed him.

"You don't seriously think we ought to go on working?"

"We've got to live in this town, Hugh!"

"For the rest of our lives!"

"It's hard enough trying to get ourselves accepted as it is."

"But if you're going to side with the enemy . . ."

"What enemy?" asked Hugh.

"Mr. Boyd and the company directors," said Colin.

"Sir Gerald bloody Fraser," said David.

"They're just human beings the same as we are," said Hugh.

"No," said David. "They are not the same as us. They are parasites, Hugh! Sitting on their fat backsides in their fancy offices and making a living from our labor. We do the work and they get rich . . . and that's how it is. Not much better than it was in Victorian times!"

"I thought you hated the job anyway," said Colin.

"No reason to go on strike though, is it?"

"So you're not going to join us?"

"You've got no hope of winning anyway," said Hugh.

There was a long silence.

A train drifted down the valley.

Dry dust blew in the wind.

"It's Helena, isn't it?" said Dilys.

"What's she got to do with it?" asked Hugh.

"She's the reason you're taking this stand! Don't want to upset her, do you? Don't want to fall out with her precious father! You should have finished with her before . . . when I told you to!"

Glenda shook her head. "That's Hugh's business, Dilys."

"Not when it affects us!" Dilys retorted. "And if he goes on working, I'm not providing him with meals! And I'm not going to live in the same house with him either! He can pack his bags and get out!"

"We agreed to stick together," Flutey said miserably.

"Tell that to Hugh!" said Dilys.

"Do we have to quarrel?" asked Glenda.

"No," said Di. "Let's at least spare ourselves that." He rose from the box on which he had been sitting. "You'd better come and stay with us, Hugh, until this thing is settled."

"Traitor!" said Colin.

"That's right," said Di. "But I've got a wife and two children to keep, see? And Hugh's right . . . you've got no bargaining power. There are thousands of unemployed people in this valley alone who will be only too glad to take our places in the colliery, and I'm not putting my job at risk for a futile gesture! Hugh and I will go to work together. And if it's strikebreaking we'll be at, then so be it."

■   ■   ■

When Helena and her mother returned from their vacation, there was a message waiting at Cardiff Central Station: Mr. Boyd was unable to meet them. They could have taken another train to Ynysceiber, but they were tired of traveling so hired a taxi instead. There were drought conditions everywhere, water rationing in all the major cities, and temperatures in South Wales were higher than the South of France. But there were no white villas and turquoise sea . . . no blue morning glory, pink oleander, or scarlet hibiscus . . . no lush greenery or shady trees. The land grew bleaker as they drove up the valley, treeless and flowerless, except for the weeds growing on the roadside verges.

Ever since she'd left, Helena had been longing to come home. But it was Hugh and the others who compelled her, not the environment. All over again the impoverishment struck her . . . dust and litter everywhere . . . ragged children playing in the streets, and men and women with hostile eyes watching the taxi go by.

For the first time ever she felt thankful she lived at Highview House, was actually glad when they arrived. The beech trees were rare and beautiful, the lawn green from constant watering. Roses bloomed in the garden and flowering clematis twined around the security fence. And the indoor coolness was a positive relief. She showered and changed, relaxed on the sofa and read a magazine. And Hugh could wait until tomorrow, she decided.

Then the telephone rang and her mother broke the news.

The miners were on strike, she said.

"Since when?" asked Helena.

"Nearly three weeks ago," Mrs. Boyd said worriedly.

"So why didn't Daddy tell us?"

"He didn't want to spoil our vacation," said Mrs. Boyd. "There was nothing we could have done about it anyway."

Angharad came in with salad and a tureen of vegetables, which she placed on the coffee table. Helena noticed her hands, rough and reddened, the cheap engagement ring that winked on one finger, and the blue cotton dress she wore, washed almost colorless.

"Shall I carve the ham, madam?"

"If you please," said Mrs. Boyd.

"None for Mr. Boyd, is it? As usual."

"He won't be home until later this evening," said Mrs. Boyd.

"If he is home at all," said Angharad. "And all he is needing to do is give the miners a decent living wage and the strike can be settled immediately. Perhaps if you could be pointing this out to him, madam . . ."

"How much each person gets paid is not my husband's decision!" Mrs. Boyd said curtly. "It's not my place to interfere in company affairs, nor is it your place to ask me, Angharad! Now go and carve the ham!"

146

Angharad pursed her lips.

"Yes, madam. Certainly, madam. Whatever you say, madam. And is it the trifle with cream you will be wanting afterward? Or the apricot torte?"

She left without waiting for an answer.

And slammed the door.

"The damned cheek of these people!" said Mrs. Boyd. "A common domestic telling me what to do!"

"I don't suppose we pay *her* a decent living wage either," said Helena. "And she made a reasonable enough request."

"Whose side are you on?" asked Mrs. Boyd.

"There shouldn't be any sides!"

"Your loyalty should be with your father!"

"You said yourself it has nothing to do with Daddy! It's company policy . . . Sir Gerald bloody Fraser!"

"But as colliery manager your father's going to be held responsible, Helena. And he needs our support."

Angharad returned with the sliced ham.

Her face was grim, her eyes hard as flint.

"I'm giving notice," she said. "As of now."

"Very well," said Mrs. Boyd.

"If I can be having my wages, please . . ."

"You can call for them in the morning," said Mrs. Boyd. "And when you leave, don't forget to put the dustbin outside the gate ready for collection."

"I don't take orders from you, madam, not anymore."

"I'm sure there are others who will be only too pleased . . ."

"Not in this valley!" said Angharad.

Then she was gone.

Helena heard her footsteps going down the drive a few moments later, and the rattle of the security gate as she

147

closed it behind her. She did not blame her. Her mother had purchased Angharad's labor, and behaved as if she owned her. Probably, thought Helena, her father and Sir Gerald Fraser felt the same about the miners, expecting them to serve and obey in exchange for wages. It *was* a kind of servitude, just as Hugh had said.

But it ought not to be, thought Helena. Angharad was a person in her own right, not just a paid slave, and they should have been grateful for everything she did. Her worth in their lives had been far more than her wages. And so was the worth of every miner to Sir Gerald Fraser. Because of them he retained his lifestyle and sailed his yacht . . . and the Boyd family lived at Highview House . . . a thousand men in Ynysceiber working to keep them.

Just for a moment Helena felt guilty. But what else was there? What other way could people survive? Without an alternative there would always be some who were better off than others, and it was hardly her fault her father was one of them. But she could not help wondering how Hugh would feel about taking a position in management, and if her father had spoken to him yet.

"We shall have to share the chores," said Mrs. Boyd.

"Maybe everything ought to be based on sharing," said Helena.

"That's very enlightened," said Mrs. Boyd.

"And if you volunteer for something, then it can't be servitude," said Helena.

"In that case you can do the cleaning and I'll do the cooking," said Mrs. Boyd. "Until we find someone to replace Angharad. You're old enough to take some responsibility for the running of the house."

"Don't spoil it, Mommy."

148

"Well, you can't expect *me* to do it all!"

"I don't," said Helena.

"When you've finished your meal, you'd better unpack your suitcases and sort out your dirty laundry."

"Stop giving me orders, will you!"

"These things have to be done, Helena."

"So why don't you try asking me instead of telling me?"

"If you weren't totally lacking in consideration, I wouldn't even need to ask, let alone tell you! And do we have to quarrel? We've hardly been home five minutes . . ."

Helena stood up.

And all over again she knew why Angharad had left.

"I'm going out!" she said.

"Where?" asked Mrs. Boyd. "And what about your dirty laundry? What about doing the dishes? I thought we agreed!"

"You know what thought did!" Helena retorted.

She left by the patio doors.

Six weeks with her mother had been almost more than she could bear. She needed the sanity of the small terraced house . . . Dilys and David and Glenda, Di and Mrs. Di, Colin and Flutey. And most of all she needed Hugh. He was wrong when he said he did not give her anything. He had introduced her to the only real happiness she had ever known.

■ ■ ■

Hugh did not really know what drove him to go on working when almost everyone else was on strike. It was some kind of perversity, maybe, a determination not to be swayed by any decision that was not his own. And he was not the only one. Apart from Di, there were twenty other miners who

149

defied the pickets . . . ignored the cat calls, the verbal abuse and threats of physical violence . . . and reported regularly for duty.

Gradually Hugh got to know them . . . older men mostly, unemployed for thirty years until the pit reopened, and stubbornly refusing to jeopardize their jobs. But there were a few nearer his own age . . . Hacker Jones, twenty-one last April, big and brawny and declining to be pushed around by anyone . . . Gwyn Griffiths, who had studied economics in a junior college and knew full well that spiraling wages led to spiraling unemployment . . . and Tom Llewellyn, whose grandmother remembered the pit strike of the nineteen eighties, the shaming of the miners, the shut-downs and job losses because of it.

There was nothing for any of them to do in the way of mining. The generator was silent, the trams lay idle, the winding wheel stopped . . . except for a daily underground check by a team of safety engineers. The miners were assigned to general maintenance . . . clearing the yard, tidying the buildings, creosoting the engine shed, painting the shower rooms and locker rooms and management offices.

Almost three weeks of deadlock passed. And the company was losing money, Mr. Boyd informed them, millions of ecu for each day the colliery was out of production. It could not go on paying them indefinitely.

"We'll be laid off, then?" asked Di.

"At the end of the month," said Mr. Boyd.

"If it's through no fault of our own, at least we'll qualify for welfare," said Gwyn Griffiths.

"I won't," said Hugh. "I'm under age."

Hacker spat in the dust.

"Best get the bastards back to work, Mr. Boyd."

"Would you like to tell me how, Mr. Jones?"

"What about an increased production bonus?" someone suggested.

"Or the bosses taking a little less and giving the miners a little more?" said Gwyn.

Mr. Boyd sighed.

"For myself I'd be willing, but I doubt if the company directors will agree to a wage cut. We'll try for the increased production bonus, I think."

He went into the office.

And Hugh followed with a can of paint.

He painted the window frames white . . . listened to a discussion between Mr. Boyd and his secretary on the impalatability of instant coffee . . . and a telephone call to Mrs. Boyd confirming she was back, had had a good vacation, and letting her know the miners were on strike . . . and another telephone call to a power station to say that future deliveries of coal would be coming from Nottingham. But there was no telephone call to the head office, no appeal on behalf of the miners for an increased production bonus. Mr. Boyd simply settled at his desk and studied the *Times* crossword.

Heat and dust drifted through the open doorway.

And Hugh began to wonder.

"You're not going to follow it up, are you Mr. Boyd?"

"Follow what up, Hugh?"

"The increased production bonus," said Hugh.

"Maybe I already know what the answer will be?"

"And that's the company policy, is it? Wait for the trickle-back effect? Do nothing and hope the miners will give up of

151

their own accord and report back for work? Good rational thinking, that is. Stands to reason they can't stay out indefinitely."

Mr. Boyd laid down his pen.

"Have you ever thought of going in for management, Hugh?"

"No," said Hugh.

"Maybe you should?"

"Wouldn't stand a chance though, would I?"

"There are certain promotional schemes available. . . ."

"I don't really think I'm management material, Mr. Boyd."

"The fact that you are working while others are striking suggests a certain keenness of attitude, and a sense of loyalty to the company. If I were to send in a personal recommendation . . ."

"It's very good of you to offer, Mr. Boyd . . ."

"You'll be based in London, of course, for the first twelve months or so. After that you'll probably be sent for training in one of our subsidiary companies abroad. South Africa, perhaps?"

"You are misunderstanding my meaning, Mr. Boyd. . . ."

"It's a great opportunity, Hugh."

"But I don't want it, see?"

Mr. Boyd stared at him.

"You don't want it?"

"No," said Hugh.

"Why not?" asked Mr. Boyd.

Hugh hesitated.

Then he told the truth.

"I don't want to set myself up, give people orders, live off their labors or wreck their lives."

"*I've* never made a practice of wrecking people's lives, Hugh."

"But you would if you had to," said Hugh. "You would if the company told you to, because that's what you're employed to do. You'd fire the lot of us if you had to. I don't want that kind of power, see? I've lived amid the wreckage of my father. I know what unemployment's like. And I couldn't do it, not to any man, no matter how much money I got paid."

Mr. Boyd leaned back in his padded chair.

"So you're content to stay at the coal face for the rest of your life?"

"I wouldn't say that," said Hugh.

"What's your alternative?"

"I don't know," said Hugh. "But there has to be one."

"Like what?" asked Mr. Boyd.

"Some kind of future that's not bound up in a decaying technological and industrial system," said Hugh. "I mean, anything that's based on nonrenewable resources isn't going to last, is it? What's going to be left when the coal runs out? How will the next generation manage? That's what I'm looking for, see? A way of life that will last. And I won't be caring how long or hard I have to work for it, how much I get out of it or what the wages will be."

He dipped his brush in the can of paint.

And continued to paint the window.

And Mr. Boyd watched him.

"You're an idealist, Hugh."

"Maybe that's what's needed, Mr. Boyd. And when the impetus doesn't come from the top, then it has to come from the bottom, see? From people like me."

"And where does my daughter fit into this vision of yours?"

Hugh paused.

White paint trickled down his fingers.

"She probably doesn't," he admitted.

"Have you told her?"

"I've tried telling her."

"Then I suggest you try harder," Mr. Boyd said quietly. "Or better still, remove yourself from the area."

Hugh turned to look at him.

"Are you giving me the push, Mr. Boyd?"

"Not exactly, son. Let's say I'm making you an offer you can't refuse . . . a transfer to a colliery in Yorkshire as soon as I can arrange it. On full wages, of course."

■ ■ ■

Nothing had changed in the small backyard, except the expressions on their faces . . . confused and wary, as if they had not expected Helena to come there. For a moment no one spoke. The baby slept in her cradle, and Glenda rocked her. Flutey scraped potatoes into a saucepan by his feet, and Dilys simply stared at her, fierce blue eyes narrowed against the light. Something was wrong . . . Helena could feel it.

"Where's . . . ?"

"Colin and David are on picket duty," said Glenda.

"And Hugh is no longer living here," said Dilys.

"He's sleeping on Di's sofa," said Flutey.

"Why?" asked Helena.

"You really don't know?" asked Dilys.

"I only arrived home a couple of hours ago," said Helena.

"There's a strike," said Dilys.

"Daddy said that much over the phone."

"And Hugh's still working," said Glenda.

"He's a scab!" Dilys said bitterly. "And Di is too! Both of them licking your father's boots!"

Helena stared at them, not knowing what to say. It had to be her fault Hugh was making a stand. Her father must have said something to him . . . offered him a career in management . . . which made it impossible for him to go on strike. It must have been awful, she thought, having to chose between his future and his friends. And then it was her turn. Their voices challenged her.

"You can come in if you want to."

"You'll still be welcome, see?"

"We won't be holding it against you."

"What Hugh does is his business."

"And you don't have to agree with him."

"I like the color of your sundress."

"Did you have a nice vacation?"

"Come and tell us about it."

"Unless you'd rather go to Number Thirty-five, of course?"

"Keep Mrs. Di company?"

"Wait for Hugh to come home?"

Helena chewed her lip. And Dilys smiled, and Glenda watched her, and Flutey peeled potatoes . . . waiting for her to choose between them and Hugh. If she chose Hugh, they would no longer be there for her, her visits no longer welcome. What Helena felt was a terrible grief as she turned on her heel and walked away.

Mrs. Di led her inside, gave her a handkerchief to wipe her eyes, shooed William and Olwen from the kitchen, poured homemade lemonade into a cracked tumbler. Quite simply, Helena did not understand how the others could behave like

155

that, how they could turn against Hugh and herself and Di and Mrs. Di, over nothing more than a difference of opinion. But differences of opinion had been the cause of every war since time began, Mrs. Di said grimly, as if those who differed were no longer human.

"That's exactly what I liked about them," Helena said brokenly. "They actually accepted me as a human being. And now they don't, even though I'm still the same person."

"You've got Hugh and me and Di, *cariad*."

"But it's not the same," said Helena.

"No," said Mrs. Di. "It's not the same. All the good that was between us is spoiled and gone. Friend is turned against friend, family against family. Hugh and Di are criminal, and we are social outcasts by association. Insane it is, to my way of thinking. Insane the world that gives rise to such a situation."

"Isn't there anything we can do?" asked Helena.

Mrs. Di sighed.

"I am not liking it any more than you are. But as Di is so fond of saying . . . you cannot be changing other people . . . you can only be changing yourself. And if you are changing yourself for the better, then so, too, will the world. And maybe it will, one day. Maybe we'll find a way of living peaceably together in spite of our differences. But I doubt if it will be in Ynysceiber!"

"Don't you like it here?" Helena asked her.

"It is not what I was hoping for," said Mrs. Di. "Worse than Cardiff, really, because I am not knowing anyone to speak to and we are not much better off. But what else is there? It is the same choice between bad wages or welfare wherever you go . . . although Hugh has his dreams."

"How is he?" Helena asked softly.

156

"Grieved," said Mrs. Di. "The same as the rest of us."

In the yard her children quarreled.

And there were too many losses for Helena to bear.

She stood up to go.

Then the back gate rattled . . . William shrieked . . . she heard Hugh and Di talking . . . and Olwen came running into the house. They were all dirty and smelly, and they needed a scrubbing brush and a bowl of water, Olwen said.

"And some clean clothes!" shouted Di.

"What's going on?" asked Mrs. Di.

She went outside and Helena followed her. They stood in the yard, human shapes that were Hugh and Di. They were covered in slurry . . . their clothes, their hair, their faces. Only their eyes showed through . . . Di's twinkling blue . . . and Hugh's gray as cloud, gazing at Helena as she gazed at him. William found a watering can, and conversations happened around them, but Hugh and Helena might have been alone.

"You're back then?" he said.

"Yes," said Helena.

"No wealthy Frenchman in tow?"

"No," said Helena.

"Bit of a wasted trip then, wasn't it?"

"I told you it would be," said Helena.

She wanted to hug him.

But the stink was strong and obnoxious.

And she helped him unbutton his shirt.

"What happened?"

"Pickets," he told her. "Colin and David in particular. They were waiting for us. With two buckets of sheep shit mixed with water."

"I hope it made them happy," Helena replied.

157

12

Hugh did not want to feel the way he did about Helena. He did not want to care. Yet he did, in spite of himself. After six weeks of absence it was almost like seeing her for the first time . . . a twist of his emotions, a constant noticing. Or maybe it was the last time he would see her, so the emotions were the same, acute and poignant, and he needed to notice her in order to remember.

She was clean and golden in the shadows of the house. She wore a dress the color of ripe apricots and white strap sandals, and her skin was tanned, her long hair bleached by the sun. He noticed the blue of her eyes, and the scent of flowers when she moved. He noticed her smile, her laughter, the intonations of her voice. And all the while he was aware that she did not belong there amid the tatty furniture, and the children chattering, and the smells of fries and sausage, with Di and Mrs. Di and in his life.

She stayed for the evening meal, and talked about her

vacation . . . breakfasts taken on a terrace overlooking the
sea, mornings spent in the hotel swimming pool, wind-
surfing and bus tours, dinners in restaurants and leisurely
drinks in sidewalk cafes, palm trees and flowers. It was all
a million miles away from Ynysceiber, the dust in the streets
and the miners' strike, the August heat and a sense of be-
reavement she failed to understand. She was sorry, of
course, about Dilys and Colin and Flutey. She was sorry
about David and Glenda, too. But her connection with them
was different from Hugh's, the rejection far less personal.
In a few short hours, knowing she was welcome in Mrs. Di's
house, Helena had made up for the loss.

But Hugh never would. Their friendship went back a long
way . . . with Dilys and Colin and Flutey in particular . . .
all the way back to childhood. Walking with Helena up the
lane to Highview House, seeing them beneath him in the small
backyard, hearing snatches of their voices and the baby's cry,
made him realize he had lost his continuity, lost touch with
his past. Ynysceiber had grown meaningless without them,
and the future was unimaginable, containing no one but himself. And Helena's transitory touch gave him no comfort.

"I wonder how they're managing without any money,"
she mused.

"Stewed bones and stinging nettles?" Hugh suggested.

"But that's awful!"

"It's their choice, isn't it?"

"Maybe if I took them some groceries . . . ?"

"They probably wouldn't accept."

Helena sighed. "I don't understand what they hope to
achieve. I mean they can't possibly win . . . and there's
nothing Daddy can do if the company digs its heels in. Has
he spoken to you yet?"

"Earlier on today," said Hugh.

"So what did he say?"

"He offered me a transfer to a colliery in Yorkshire," said Hugh. "An offer, he said, that I couldn't refuse."

Helena stared at him.

The hills were black and silver above her.

And the moonlight shone in her eyes.

Her voice was wild.

"My father said that? The double-crossing swine! I'll kill him! He's worse than my mother! At least she's never pretended to be anything else!"

"It's just his way of trying to protect you from me," said Hugh.

"I hope you told him to shove it?"

"I told him I'd think about it."

"Surely you don't want to go to Yorkshire?"

"No," said Hugh. "But I don't want to be unemployed either."

"So you'll go then?"

"If I want to eat I've got no choice, have I?"

"You can't let Daddy push you around!"

"Whoever pays the piper . . ."

"So what about me? What about us?"

"It had to happen sometime, didn't it?"

"You can't just leave, Hugh!"

"What else is there, Helena?"

"There's got to be something!" Helena said desperately.

"That's what I thought once," said Hugh. "I thought if I had a job, everything would be all right. But it isn't. It's turned into a trap I can't get out of. If I was old enough to claim welfare, it might be different. At least I'd have a kind of choice. Now, in order to survive, I have to do what your father and the British Mining Company tell me to do. They've got me over a barrel, Helena, and there *is* nothing else. So we may as well forget about us."

"No!" wailed Helena.

"I'm sorry, *cariad*."

"We can work something out! I know we can!"

"We can't fight the whole flaming system, Helena! I told you before. We're living in two different worlds, and there's nothing we can do about it."

"But we love each other, Hugh!"

"That's the problem . . . but what's the solution?"

"I've got a savings account . . ."

"Which is yours, not mine," said Hugh.

"But you can't just leave me!"

"It's for your own good, see?"

"Now you sound like my bitching mother!"

"Yes," said Hugh. "She cares about you too, and your Da as well. It's where you belong, see? With them, not with me."

He left her by the gate, turned up the track beside the barn, ignored her when she screamed his name and hoped she would not follow. He knew she must hurt as badly as he did, but there was nothing he could do about it. The British Mining Company had stripped him of his options, destroyed his hope. In exchange for a job he hated and one hundred ecu a week he had lost everything, been deprived of Helena and sacrificed his friends. Only the hills remained, black and silver, endless miles of loneliness.

■ ■ ■

Helena had trusted her father, but she would never trust him again, nor would she ever forgive him for what he had

161

done. She screamed at him in all her hurt and anger, everything hidden being heaved to the surface, bitter accusations that were hurled back at her. She had been stupid to pick on someone like Hugh in the first place, said Mr. Boyd. And he had done what he could, offered him a chance of promotion, but Hugh turned it down. He was a loser, said Mr. Boyd, totally lacking in drive, or ambition, or any other quality that would enable him to succeed in the cutthroat world of business. He would never get anywhere because he did not want to, and there was no way Mr. Boyd was going to recommend him.

"So you stabbed him in the back!" screeched Helena.

"I offered him a transfer to Yorkshire, that's all."

"It's for your own good," said Mrs. Boyd.

That was what Hugh had said.

But how did he know what was good for her?

And how did her parents know?

Hating them both, she went upstairs and slammed the bedroom door. She was sick of other people's opinions. Her mother had been nagging her for weeks, months, ever since Hugh had come to Ynysceiber. She was sick of all the justifying, and persuading, and appealing to her reasoning. It was not Helena's reasoning at all . . . it was her mother's view of things she was expected to accept and comply with. Now her father had sided against her. And it never occurred to either of them to ask what Helena thought and felt, or what she wanted.

And it had never occurred to her either, she thought. She had always assumed that Hugh wanted what she did . . . but she had never asked him. Instead she had tried to arrange things for him, manipulate him into accepting what she

162

thought was best for both of them, connived with her father as now her father connived against her.

Hugh was a loser, Mr. Boyd had said. He would never get anywhere because he did not want to. And he had turned down an offer of promotion. Why? wondered Helena. How could he do that? How could he refuse the chance of success? Status, and money, and possessions, and everything else that went with it? If he had accepted, then he and Helena might have had a future together. Her parents would have been for them, instead of against them. But he had turned it down, turned *her* down, rejected her along with her whole way of life.

Bitter tears ran down her face.

And she wiped them away on the hem of her skirt.

She did not understand him. How could he choose to be a loser? How could anyone choose it? Yet compared to Mr. Boyd most people were losers, she thought, the miners at the coal face and the millions of unemployed. The world could not support success for very many. There were not the resources anymore. So the majority had to be losers, at least in the material sense. But they hardly chose it, not as Hugh had done, deliberately, on principle, out of some perverse sense of pride.

He must be mad, she thought.

He must be out of his mind.

Yet she knew he was not.

It was one of the reasons she liked him . . . because he was sane. He had other qualities too. He was kind and honest, and loyal to his friends, capable of enduring all kinds of hardship and deprivations, and resourceful enough to rescue her from a riot.

163

And in the colliery he worked long hours for lousy wages, and refused to go on strike. As a human being he was not a loser at all . . . no more than Di was, or David was, or Glenda, Dilys, Colin or Flutey . . . no more than Mrs. Price or Angharad or anyone else.

Not our kind, Mrs. Boyd said of them. And she was right, thought Helena. Ordinary people were not dependent on a fat income and a luxury lifestyle to the detriment of everyone else. But recognizing that, could Helena turn away from the life she had been born to and live as they did? Could she give up her innerspring mattress for a bed of heather? Cook on a fire, like Mrs. Di? Give birth in an upstairs bedroom like Glenda had? Or be like Dilys, not caring about what she wore or how she looked? Could she choose to share their poverty, as Hugh had done?

She already knew the answer.

And a loneliness touched her, too deep for tears.

Downstairs the telephone rang, and her father answered it. She heard voices talking on the television. And outside she heard an owl hoot, the bleat of sheep on the hills, and a breath of wind that rustled the leaves of the beech trees by the barn. She walked to the window, saw the night sky bright with stars and the lights of the houses in the valley, sensed the grievances of a community that she could never share.

She and Hugh did not live in two different worlds, she thought sadly. They lived in the same world, both of them part of a human society that was neither fair nor just. There were the haves and the have-nots, the privileged few and the impoverished many, a manmade division neither she nor Hugh could cross. In truth, she could no more accept Hugh's kind of life than he could accept hers. So they had

164

no future together. And if they loved each other at all, they would have to let each other go.

■ ■ ■

Hugh sat among the crags. He sat there for several hours watching the lights wink out in the valley beneath him, hearing an owl hoot in the distance and sheep chewing their cud in the silence nearby. He had come there often during the last weeks, seeking an escape from what he felt, the terrible separateness from Dilys and Colin and Flutey, Mrs. Di's unhappiness and Helena's absence, and now the ending between them.

It had had to happen, he thought.

For her sake it had had to happen.

But it could have been different . . . if he had gone along with her father, accepted his offer of promotion and kept his mouth shut. If he was doing things for Helena's sake, he should have gone for the power and the money, risen above his background and paid no attention to those who had once been his friends. He could have made annual donations to charity to ease his conscience, as Mr. Boyd did, sent money orders to his mother, bought a detached house and employed domestics, helped people out in a far more practical way. As it was, he had fouled up the chance of a lifetime and gained nothing.

He must have been mad, he thought.

He must have been totally stupid.

But how could he accept a solution for himself that was not available to anyone else? That kind of lifestyle, and all that Mr. Boyd offered and Helena wanted, was wrong. It had always been wrong . . . based on a fallacy: the rape of the earth they believed could go on forever. It sprang from

165

an illusion gone rampant in the twentieth century of perpetual economic growth and increased wealth for everyone. It was a fool's paradise, and for Hugh to become part of it, he would have to turn his back on his own experiences and blind himself to the truth.

He knew natural resources were running out. He knew all jobs were temporary that depended on a finite source of energy. He knew that the whole infrastructure of industrial civilization was gradually collapsing. And in the future, when the remaining coal was mined out, then where would he be? Unemployed yet again, with years of his life wasted on work he hated, and the earth impoverished even more because of him.

He did not want to be part of all that. He did not want to go to Yorkshire and do what Mr. Boyd wanted him to do. But if he refused, he would probably be fired, lose his job and have to live on nothing. Unless he gave in his notice anyway? Returned to Cardiff and stayed with his parents? Or took to the hills, built a hut of stones, and lived on rabbits and berries?

He raised his head.

Black and silver, the hills slept beneath the moonlight. No one could live up here, Helena had said. But maybe she was wrong. Maybe people could live up here and all it took was courage. And when there was nothing else, the land remained, the world of the owl and the sheep and the stars—rich and potent as it had always been, not just for him but for everyone.

He remembered the history he had learned in school. Once, in their millions, people had left the land to work in the cities. But now the cities offered nothing anymore, so maybe, instinctively, they would return to the land.

Suddenly Hugh could sense it, the slow whittling down of alternatives, the enforced exodus of which he was a forerunner.

There was hope out here, he thought, in places like this, amid the grass and soil, peat bogs and heather. Small ferns shivered in the crevices of the crags. He could feel the untamed wildness that was all about him.

The earth had survived in spite of all the poison and pollution, the wastage of cities and the concrete poured over it, the damage of intensive farming. It had survived in spite of all the human race had done.

It stirred a longing inside him, a kind of love that was almost holy. But he did not know what to do about it, or how to answer it.

Maybe, he thought, it was not for him at all. Not for his generation, but for those who would come after him, for Di's children and little Rhiannon, the new beginning of a new age. But it was something to know that things were not entirely hopeless. It gave him a sense of direction, a hint maybe of what he ought to do and where he ought to go.

He rose from his seat.

And then he saw them . . . come there mysteriously and set loose on the hillside: beasts in the moonlight, tossing their heads and kicking up their heels. The sheep scattered as the shrill whinnying of horses filled the night. Hooves thundered on dry ground as they galloped up the open slope, magnificent symbols that seemed to endorse his thinking. He watched them charge toward the skyline, toward the unfettered freedom of the land from which he, and most human beings, had turned away.

And he wondered who had led them there, who had released them. No one in Ynysceiber owned horses, except for the milkman down the valley who kept a single piebald to pull the delivery van. He saw shadows that were people heading back along the lane toward the town, three or four of them, strangers who had arrived unannounced in the middle of the night as once he had done. Looking for jobs, were they? A few more hopes about to be shattered? Or did they have another, different purpose?

Hugh did not know.

And he could not guess.

But he followed them down the hill toward Di's sofa.

■   ■   ■

After her parents went to bed, at twenty to midnight by the clock radio, Helena heard the soft neighing of a horse and a clatter of hooves coming up the lane. Curious, and needing a distraction from her own miserable thoughts, she crept from her room, opened the landing window and leaned out. Moonlight shone on the gravel yard, on the roofs of the outbuildings and on the hills beyond. And someone was there, people and horses going up the track beside the paddock.

Helena remembered the riding lessons she had had as a child. That awful horsey stage, her mother called it. But for Helena it had been the happiest time of her life. Each Saturday, with a friend named Deborah, she used to go to the local stables. In the mornings they helped clean the tack and shovel dung from the stalls. And in the afternoons they rode along a bridle path through the woods, or across the open downs. She remembered the sun on her face and the wind in her hair, the chestnut power of the breath and muscle, herself and the horse riding in relationship.

Strange how much she had loved it, she thought, wading through churned mud to open gates, smashing ice on the horse troughs in winter, and the rank animal smells that clung to her clothes. She had been a child in touch with a much more natural world, alive to the landscape in all its seasons and the horse that carried her through it. Then the stables went bankrupt and the horses were sold. Deborah took up tap dancing and Helena grew out of her jodhpurs and hat and never went riding again.

But it might be nice to own a horse, she thought. There was room here . . . a paddock to keep it in . . . and they could convert one of the garages back into a stable. It would be nice to ride across the hills, something to look forward to, something to come home for from the university . . . a horse to fill the emptiness without Hugh.

Once again the tears prickled her eyes. But she blinked them away, watched as the horses reached the top of the track and were released. They were far away but she caught the joy of their whinnying, saw them kick up their heels and gallop away . . . horses, wild in the moonlight, heading toward the sky.

Then they were gone, and the men turned homeward, the hill slope silvery above them, and the crags black and solid on the high horizon. But suddenly Helena saw movement, a darkness that separated from the darkness of stone and became a person. She knew him at once. Small and distant, solitary beneath a crowd of stars, Hugh picked his way between clumps of gorse and rushes down a path of pale grass.

Her heart thudded uncomfortably. He must have been up there all the time, as sleepless as she was and equally alone. If she were quick, she thought, she could put on her clothes

and go out and join him, and all would be right again between them, as if nothing had ever happened. It was strong
as an instinct, sharp as longing, an inner prompting urging
her to obey . . . disregard everything she had previously
thought and decided. She fought against it, her knuckles
whitening as she gripped the windowsill. Then, for her own
good, she turned and went back to bed.

13

Hugh and Di made beet sandwiches and left the house early, at a quarter to seven, to avoid the pickets. The milkman, with his horse, was still making deliveries and the day was already hot. But the hills were hazy. There was a hint of autumn in the air and mist above the river. And in the parking lot, where the market was held, was a huddle of horse-drawn caravans. They were colorful as houseboats Hugh had once seen in a travel brochure . . . maroon with swirls of gilding at their eaves, or green or blue with brightly painted flowers on their sides.

"Gypsies," said Di.

"Or new age travelers," said Hugh.

"Too tidy," said Di.

"Gypsies then," said Hugh.

"And what are they doing here in Ynysceiber?" asked Di.

"Just passing through?" suggested Hugh.

"Which is what anyone would do if they had any sense," said Di.

"You are not liking it here either?"

Di sighed.

"Once I was thinking it would be the answer, see? It is what we had dreamed of, me and Mrs. Di . . . a secure life with a real job, having a place in a community and watching the children grow. But it's not like that in Ynysceiber. Incomers we are, and we are not much better off than we were on welfare. And what will there be for William and Olwen, we are asking? It is the same unemployment waiting for them here as there was in Cardiff, and the same temptations. I am seeing it going on . . . the drugs and the sex and the loud music."

"Stops them thinking about things," said Hugh.

"But I fear for them, see?"

"William might get a job in the pit."

"No solution though, is it?" said Di.

"How do you mean?" asked Hugh.

"We are still dependent," said Di. "We are as dependent on wages as we were on welfare. Working in the pit is not increasing our freedom but decreasing it."

"That's what I feel," said Hugh.

"And we are not working for our own benefit either," said Di. "Nor to the benefit of people in general. Who benefits most from our labors are the likes of Mr. Boyd and the company directors. I've been thinking about it a lot lately. The strike will be changing nothing, and never has. It is the whole employment system that is needing to be changed. What work a man does should be in his own hands, of his own choosing, for rewards of his own making and not just money."

Their pit boots struck sparks from the street. And a crowd of swallows had gathered on the telephone wires, poised to fly southward. It was easy for them, thought Hugh. They were unencumbered and found their food on the wing. Easy for the Gypsies, too. They went where they would and their homes went with them.

"Maybe we ought to leave," said Hugh.

"And where would we go?" asked Di. "If here is the same as Cardiff, where else would be different? And who will welcome us?"

"I don't know," said Hugh. "But I'll be damned if I'm going to Yorkshire because Mr. Boyd tells me to for the sake of his daughter. When I leave Ynysceiber, it's going to be for positive reasons, not a shift in scenery and more of the same."

"Well, be sure to let me know when you find something," said Di. "I'll be right there with you along with Mrs. Di and the kids."

"I'll hold you to that," said Hugh.

■   ■   ■

The houses ended and the road led on across the empty hillside to the colliery. Below, a single-track railway branched from the main line to the loading sheds, its rails already rusting from lack of use. The coal stocks were gone, nothing left but wheel ruts in acres of blackened earth, and the slag heap towering above the buildings. Sunlight glinted on the security fence that surrounded the site.

The wire gates rattled as they opened and closed them. And they were not the first to arrive. Mr. Boyd's blue Mercedes was already parked outside his office, and his secretary's bicycle was propped against the wall. They heard the hiss of the photocopier through the open door, making use of the two hours of electricity available. They heard the clatter of the manual typewriter. Mr. Boyd tapped on the window as they passed and beckoned them inside.

"You're early," he said.

"A bid for self-preservation," said Di.

"Well, it won't be for much longer," said Mr. Boyd. "The men will be back to work by the end of the week. And those that aren't . . ."

He ran a hand across his throat.

"You will be giving them the ultimatum?" asked Hugh.

"Nine hundred and seventy-nine of them," said Mr. Boyd.

Rhythmically he fed the photocopier, gathered up the printed sheets and pointed to the pile of envelopes on his desk that were already addressed.

"The letters will be going out today," he said. "One for every employee of the company who has chosen to go on strike. Each single sheet needs to be folded and sealed into its respective envelope. Later we'll work out a delivery schedule."

"You mean you are wanting us to do it?" asked Hugh.

"Do you have any objections?" asked Mr. Boyd.

Hugh shrugged and picked up one of the letters.

It was brief and to the point.

In compliance with instructions from Headquarters, I am hereby informing you that the strike action you are presently involved in will no longer be tolerated. Unless you return to work by the end of this present week, accepting a renegotiated contract and reduced wages, you will no longer be considered an employee of this Company. And the vacancy

174

created by you will be readvertised and filled from outside
your immediate locality.

It was signed at the bottom by Mr. Boyd's name.

He would fire them all if he had to.

And Hugh, for money, was expected to collude . . . lick and seal the envelopes containing nine hundred and seventy-nine threats of defeat and dismissal, and help deliver them to his fellow men. Dependent on the company, they would likely do as they were told . . . return to work, every last one of them, having no alternative and no appeal.

"This isn't my job," said Hugh.

"It is if you want to go on working for the company," said Mr. Boyd.

"If you separate need from desire, I doubt if anyone *wants* to," said Hugh.

"Too bloody right!" said Di.

"And certainly not for reduced wages," said Hugh.

Mr. Boyd shrugged.

"If you care to hand in your letters of resignation, I'm willing to accept them at any time."

■　■　■

It was almost eleven o'clock when Helena came downstairs. Her face was blotchy from last night's crying and she had not slept very much. The house seemed silent and empty, hollow as the life that lay ahead of her. And without Hugh, maybe she did not want to live at all. She picked up a letter lying on the hall mat, glanced at it indifferently, and went through to the kitchen.

Her mother was there, sitting at the breakfast bar, flicking through the pages of a fashion magazine. She was wearing

175

her pink velvet dressing gown and slippers, and a pair of dark glasses. She neither glanced at Helena nor spoke, her silence sharp and pointed as a punishment for last night's outrage. But Helena had no intention of apologizing, nor was she going to admit her mother might be right. Instead she helped herself to granola and raspberry yogurt, put the kettle to boil on the scarlet stove and opened the letter.

It had been sent on to her from the school in Kent . . . her examination passes . . . except that she had failed to pass them. She stared disbelievingly, but the results remained. She had failed to qualify for university or polytechnic, an academic nonstarter. Outside, the sunlight beat on the gravel yard, swallows perched on the roof ridge of the stable block and the geraniums on the windowsill wilted from lack of water. But Helena turned cold, gripped by dismay.

What would she do now? she thought. What sort of job could she hope to get without qualifications? Mundane office work? A salesclerk in a fashion boutique? Hairdressing perhaps? Crummy work for crummy wages . . . and then only if she was lucky. Whatever jobs were going, preference was always given to male applicants . . . and usually hundreds of people applied for the same post. She could even end up a domestic, as Angharad had done. And really her future prospects were no better than Hugh's. Unless she continued to live with her parents? Or married the first man with a bank account who came her way?

"There's no point in standing there waiting," Mrs. Boyd said suddenly.

"What?" said Helena.

"The stove's not lit. Angharad's left us, remember? And I don't feel up to lighting it this morning. If you want coffee, you'll have to use the camp stove. And would you mind

176

handing me a glass of water and a couple of aspirin, please? I have the most dreadful headache."

Helena ran the tap.

"Too much dry sherry, I suppose?"

"It's stress," said Mrs. Boyd. "When you think what happened yesterday, it's not surprising . . . all that traveling to get home . . . and Angharad giving notice . . . and then that awful row last night. I really don't think I can take any more. And I've never known your father to be so upset."

"It was *his* fault!" said Helena.

"That's not what I'm referring to," said Mrs. Boyd.

"So what are you referring to?"

"The phone call from Sir Gerald Fraser."

"What phone call?"

"He phoned last night," said Mrs. Boyd. "After you went storming off to bed. The company directors don't like the way your father has handled the strike situation. They want the miners back at work by the end of the week, and they won't be offering him the management of the second colliery. We're being transferred to Yorkshire instead. Yorkshire, for God's sake!"

She swallowed the tablets.

And just for a moment Helena wanted to laugh.

"Now you know how Hugh feels," she said brutally.

"It's not the same for him," said Mrs. Boyd. "His sort can fit in anywhere, but I can't. Living here is bad enough. There's no one of my own kind I can relate to. But at least I can drive to Bristol occasionally, or go shopping in Cardiff. Yorkshire's miles from anywhere . . . all moors and black pudding! Your father will be at work all day . . . you'll be away at the university . . . and I'll be on my own. It's not something to look forward to, I can tell you. And it's pretty

177

shabby treatment for someone who's given the company twenty-five years of loyal service!"

Helena could have told her mother then that she had failed her exams and would not be going to the university. But she did not want to go to Yorkshire any more than Mrs. Boyd did . . . not even on the off chance of seeing Hugh. She poked, miserably, at the dish of granola. It was as if the whole world were collapsing around her, as if nothing were stable or dependable anymore. Conventional employment seemed to offer nothing but insecurity and disappointment, she thought. No matter what job you had, you could never escape the fear of losing it, and the wages were seldom enough. Maybe it was better to be unemployed, accept the poverty and just not care anymore?

She pushed away her dish.

"If you don't want to go to Yorkshire, Daddy could always hand in his notice," she said.

Her mother looked at her.

The dark glasses robbed her of expression.

But her voice was scathing.

"Don't be so ridiculous!" she said.

■　■　■

The strike had been doomed from the start. It was the wrong economic climate to make demands. There were too many people, worse off than the miners, who were willing and eager to take their places. Mr. Boyd was expecting a one-hundred-percent return to work before the weekend.

"Bastard!" said Hacker.

"He's just doing his job," said Gwyn.

"But we're doing his dirty work!" said Hacker.

"That's what I object to," said Hugh.

178

"I thought for a moment you were going to tell him to shove it," said Di.

"I almost did," said Hugh.

"So what stopped you?" asked Gwyn.

"You know what stopped him," said Hacker. "We all know what stopped him. The same that stops all of us from telling him to shove the whole bloody coal mine!"

"Fear of unemployment," said Gwyn.

"As if any job is better than no job," Hacker said bitterly.

"I'm beginning to wonder about that," said Di.

"But what else is there?" asked Hacker.

It was early afternoon. The heat was stifling, not a breath of air anywhere, and no one about except half a dozen youths sniffing glue in a derelict garage. Glazed eyes watched them as they passed, and music blared from a portable tape deck.

"Fucking hopeless," said Hacker.

"*They* need something else as well," said Di.

"And the government's no bloody use," said Hacker.

"They don't have the funds," said Gwyn.

"God helps those who help themselves," said Hugh.

"Yes?" said Hacker. "Well, He's no bloody use either!"

They went in groups to deliver Mr. Boyd's circular, enough to protect each other in case of trouble, knocking on doors and working their way along the roads of terraced houses toward the High Street. And others besides them were spread out across the town . . . along the valley toward Abercwm, and in the public housing developments. No one welcomed them. They were seen as scabs in cahoots with the management . . . harbingers of defeat and reduced wages. And reactions varied from abuse and anger to bitter acceptance.

"Enjoying it, are you?" one miner asked them.

"No more than you," replied Hacker.

"You haven't lost what we've lost, boy!"

"We get a wage cut too," said Di.

"But yours is not the climb down!" said the miner.

"Maybe not," Di admitted.

"No pride you had to begin with, see?"

A gobbet of spittle smacked in the dust at Hugh's feet. He kept trying to tell himself he had done nothing to be ashamed of, but with each encounter he grew less and less convinced. And a general return to work was not something he, or any of those with him, could look forward to. The miners had long memories, said Gwyn, and their refusal to strike would be neither forgiven nor forgotten.

"Things could be very uncomfortable," said Gwyn.

"Maybe we should have gone along with them?" said Hugh.

"It's a bit late for that," said Di.

"They were daft to take strike action in the first place," said Gwyn. "The economic climate being what it is, it always was a futile gesture."

"We'll have to make sure we stick together," said Di.

"Look out for each others' backs," said Hacker.

"That's no way to live," said Hugh.

"We've got no choice," said Gwyn.

"I'd like to get out of this damned valley," said Hacker.

"Ditto," said Hugh.

But that, too, was a dream that seemed hopeless. They were all trapped, thought Hugh. They turned into the High Street. The secondhand clothes shop had almost nothing in it, and a notice in the grocery store said No Credit. The For Sale signs were gray with dust. Everything was gray . . . gray houses, gray walls, gray wood beneath the peeling

180

paintwork. And outside the post office the stamp machines and telephone booths were permanently vandalized. The place got to him, ground him down. Then when he glanced at the address on the next envelope, his rage exploded. His clenched fist slammed against the nearest streetlight.

"That's it!" howled Hugh.

"What's the matter?" asked Gwyn.

"That's the last flaming straw!"

"What is?" asked Di.

"Mr.Boyd has given us Bethesda Street!" said Hugh.

"That significant, is it?" asked Hacker.

"We live there," said Di.

Hugh turned to face them . . . Gwyn and Hacker, Di with his bald pate shining in the sunlight. His split knuckles bled but he felt no pain. There was a strange calmness inside him, a kind of strength and certainty devoid of any emotion, as if, for the first time in his life, he knew exactly what to do.

"There's no way I'm going to deliver these letters," he stated. "Not to Colin and Flutey and David . . . not for one hundred ecu a week nor thirty pieces of silver. I just won't do it, see?"

Slowly, deliberately, he tore them to shreds.

And dropped them in the gutter.

■　■　■

Their voices were quiet, and not unkind.

"Friends of yours, are they?"

"They were," Hugh said bitterly.

"They're not going to thank you if you lose them their jobs, are they?"

"They've got a right to know what's what, see?"

181

"You can't be deciding for them, can you?"

"They've got to make up their own minds what to do."

Di picked up the scraps of paper.

"We're going to have to tell them, Hugh."

"I can't do it, Di!"

"No," said Hacker. "No, all right."

"We'll tell them for you," said Gwyn. "What's the address?"

"I'll come with you," said Di.

Hugh leaned against the post-office wall. He felt sick with himself. He would have felt sick whatever he had done, whether he had delivered those letters or not. The sun beat on his face, rebounded from the street and the gray walls of buildings. A shabby woman with two shabby children came from the grocery store, the man in the secondhand furniture shop stood in the doorway waiting for customers. Flies buzzed on a pile of dog shit on the pavement.

Hugh closed his eyes. Patches of green light floated through the darkness inside his head. But there was no escape, he thought, no escape from the ugliness of Ynysceiber or himself.

"Are you all right?"

Her voice disturbed him, an English accent similar to Helena's. But she was shorter, plumper than Helena, and several years older . . . a girl with corn-colored hair and hazel eyes . . . regarding him inquiringly. He noticed her clothes: a sleeveless top of unbleached cloth tied at the shoulders, a long patchwork skirt in soft unusual shades of muted green, mauve and ocher, rope-soled sandals. And she carried a basket, laden with wholemeal flour, fresh vegetables and soy milk.

"Are you all right?" she repeated.

182

"Yes," said Hugh.

"I thought you were sick or something."

"It'll pass," said Hugh.

"Can I help in any way? I can't offer you a fix, but I can offer a cup of dandelion coffee and a sympathetic ear."

"I'm not an addict," said Hugh.

The girl smiled. "You can never tell these days."

"I suppose not," said Hugh.

"The offer still stands," said the girl. "Dandelion coffee or herb tea if you'd prefer it. Our caravans are down there, by the river."

Hugh looked at her suspiciously.

She was obviously no Gypsy.

"If you're some kind of religious evangelist out to save my soul, I'm not interested," he informed her.

"I'm not," she said. "Honestly, I'm not. Some of us do have spiritual leanings, but not of the orthodox kind. I promise I won't mention God, or try and convert you."

"In that case I'll carry your basket," said Hugh.

The girl relinquished her burden.

"You're unemployed, I take it?"

"No," said Hugh. "But right now I'd like to be."

"Most people would give their eyeteeth . . ."

"Obviously I'm not most people."

"So what kind of work do you do?"

"I work in the pit."

"And is it the job itself you object to?"

"I'd probably object to any kind of job."

"You mean you don't want to work at all?"

"That's not what I said."

The girl nodded.

Her plump face had grown red from the heat.

"You're open to suggestions then?"

"Are you trying to seduce me or something?"

She laughed.

"It's all quite proper," she told him. "We're an alternative-careers service, sponsored by the government. My name's Faith, by the way."

"And I'm Hugh," said Hugh.

14

Mrs. Boyd's headache got worse. She had to go to bed and draw the curtains. And Helena telephoned the doctor. He came from Abercwm, diagnosed migraine, and gave her an injection. It probably *was* stress induced, he said. And if stress came from being married to a man with a good job, having a plush house and plenty of money, then maybe Helena would be better off without. Or so she told herself, as her mother vomited and slept.

Alone in the kitchen she tried to think how she could live and what she could do with her life. But her thoughts led nowhere, and the silence depressed her, and her sense of loneliness grew acute as despair. She needed company, someone to talk things over with, someone to care. But everyone she knew in Ynysceiber was connected with Hugh . . . Glenda and Dilys cold-shouldering her because

185

of him, and Mrs. Di providing a sanctuary Helena could no longer visit. She was barred by her own emotions, afraid to run the risk of meeting him again, afraid she might cry, make a fool of herself. And where else was there to go? Only the hills where no one was . . . a loneliness greater than her own.

Then she remembered the horses. She would go and look for them. It was something to do, a temporary purpose, better than sitting here brooding. She changed into denim shorts and a sun top, smoothed sunscreen on her skin for protection against the ultraviolet light, filled her pockets with sugar lumps, and left the house.

The heat was stifling. Dry grass in the paddock brushed her legs, and the hills were hazy, tinged with purple heather. Gorse pods cracked, and thistles seeded, and flies buzzed around her eyes. She made a fan of bracken fronds and headed for the shade of the crags. But the sheep were there before her, hot wool bodies crowded together beneath the overhang. Yellow eyes glared at her resentfully, and the air was rank with their droppings. Helena veered away from them, flipped at the flies that followed her, rounded an edge of towering rock, and stopped in alarm.

Someone was sitting there, a man in his twenties, or early thirties, his long hair tied with a bootlace at the back of his neck. He wore bead earrings and strange patchwork clothes . . . a flowing shirt in soft autumnal colors, plum and russet, ocher yellow and olive green, and brown homespun trousers. His eyes were dark when he turned to look at her, and in the distance beyond him the group of horses grazed. A Gypsy, she thought, and no one to hear her however much she screamed.

Her alarm must have showed.

186

And he was quick to reassure her.

"It's okay. I'm not dangerous. I just came to check on the horses."

His voice was English.

And his smile seemed friendly enough.

Helena relaxed.

"Are they your horses?" she asked.

"Not exactly," he said. "They're just part of the team. They pull the caravans in which we live."

"But you're not a Gypsy?" said Helena.

The man smiled again.

"Nothing so exotic," he told her. "I'm a member of the alternative-careers advisory service sponsored by the government. We're parked in the parking lot by the river." He rose to his feet. "If you've come up here seeking solitude, I'll willingly push off," he said.

"No," said Helena. "I wasn't . . . I mean I'm not seeking anything. I just came to see the horses. I brought them some sugar lumps. And you don't have to go, not because of me."

Maybe he understood.

She needed someone.

"I'm Michael," he said.

"And I'm Helena," she replied.

■ ■ ■

Hugh did not need to make conversation.

Once Faith began there was no stopping her. He carried the basket, walked beside her, and listened as she talked . . . about Ynysceiber, the dilapidation, the unemployment, the lack of hope . . . and how it could be different, given effort and imagination and people working together.

Her enthusiasm was almost contagious. She had the

187

south-facing hills terraced and planted with eggplants, pep-
pers, tomatoes, corn and vines. And the north-facing hills
similarly terraced, peas and soy beans and potatoes growing
in profusion, wheat in the paddocks, and the soil enriched
with animal manures and dried human excrement. There
was a toilet system, she said, that removed the moisture
content and left a dry compost with no smell attached.

There were no animals in Ynysceiber, apart from cats and
dogs and the milkman's horse . . . but Faith had the back-
yards housing chickens, goats staked on the patches of waste-
land, and horses being used for transport. And they needed
trees, she said, in every available space . . . fruit trees and
nut bushes, willow and beech. They could have allotments
where the factories were . . . and a mill by the river . . .
and a forge . . . and a bakery. Fuel was no problem. They
could use briquettes of coal dust mixed with straw, and fix
shutters at the windows to keep in the warmth during winter. And the houses could be whitewashed in pastel colors,
with flowers grown in windowboxes and hanging baskets.

"Environment is so important," she said. "It affects people
psychologically. I mean who wants to live surrounded by
this kind of ugliness? With a little imagination it could be
totally transformed. People have to be encouraged to take
things into their own hands. The unemployed don't have to
be unemployed, you see? With training and cooperation they
can begin to improve their own lot. That's what we're here
for. And that's what we mean by alternative employment:
making your own clothes, your own baskets, your own pottery . . . building, repairing, and furnishing your own
homes, supplying your own needs, becoming an independent community, in fact."

She paused for breath in the sweltering sunlight. Her face

was flushed and her hazel eyes, fixed on Hugh, shone with a fanatical light, her own inner vision she wanted to share.

"We need someone like you, Hugh. Someone young who has drive and ambition and some intelligence to go with it. If you can whip up support and get people organized, we'll provide the backing."

Hugh could see what she was saying. He could see all of it . . . the slow rebuilding of Ynysceiber, the change in its people, the alternative way of life. Everything Faith said was sane and beautiful. She offered hope to the hopeless, creative work for all who needed it, a future for everyone.

"What do you think?" she repeated.

Hugh put down the heavy basket.

"I think it's a wonderful idea," he said.

"It has to be more than an idea," Faith said earnestly. "It has to become a reality, Hugh, and not just in Ynysceiber. We've got to create self-sufficient communities everywhere, throughout every country in Europe. We've got to utilize people's talents and abilities, get them working together, pool our resources . . ."

"You're talking about a totally different kind of society," said Hugh.

"Yes," said Faith.

"Well, as I say, it's a wonderful idea, but you don't stand a snowball's chance in hell."

She stared at him.

And the fierce brightness of her eyes faded.

Her voice sounded suddenly weary.

"We've got to try," she said. "If we don't try, things will go on getting worse. We can't depend on welfare much longer because the money is just not going to be there. We've got to do *something*, Hugh."

189

Hugh shook his head.

"They wouldn't listen to me," he said. "Not in Yny-sceiber. I'm from Cardiff, see? I'm an incomer and a scab and I'll never be part of the community. If I try for you, it can't be here—it will have to be somewhere else."

Faith nodded.

"You need to see Michael," she said.

■　■　■

Michael whistled, and the horses came to him. He patted their noses and Helena fed them sugar lumps, smelled the sweetness on their breath. They nuzzled her hands, her clothes, her face . . . horsey kisses and caresses. She had almost forgotten how strong and beautiful they were.

"They're beginning to make a comeback," said Michael.

"Some of the collieries have pit ponies," said Helena.

"They're being used on farms as well," said Michael.

"I'd like a horse," Helena said wistfully.

"For what purpose though?"

"Just to ride," said Helena.

And she saw him look at her and frown.

"Do you live in Ynysceiber?" he asked her.

"For now," said Helena. "But my mother informed me this morning we're being transferred to Yorkshire. My father works for the British Mining Company, you see, so we're obliged to go because of his job."

"But you don't want to?" Michael prompted.

"Not to Yorkshire," said Helena.

"So what will you do?"

"I don't know," said Helena. "I was going to go to the university, but I failed my exams. I heard that this morning, too."

190

"It's not your day, is it?"

"No," sighed Helena.

The horses jostled her and vied for attention. Then, when she had no more sugar lumps, they wandered away. Yet they remained, the smell of them on her clothes and in her mind the memories of her childhood, some part of her that was lost down the years, that longed to return and be recognized. She sat on the grass, rested her chin on her raised knees, and watched them. And Michael sat beside her.

"It's not the end of the world," he said.

"Isn't it?" asked Helena.

"There are plenty of alternative careers you can choose from."

"Like what?"

"Working with horses, perhaps?"

"You mean running a riding stable, or training race horses?"

Again Michael frowned. "That's not quite what I had in mind. Those kinds of leisure activities are a thing of the past, unavailable except to the lucky few. We have to begin to cater to a new social order . . . and horses are going to be a vital part of it. When the coal runs out, and the last of the oil is gone, horses are going to become our major form of transport. We're going to need farriers, horse doctors, trainers, handlers . . . to name but a few. If you're into horses, Helena, you need never be unemployed. If you come to my caravan sometime during the next week, I'll give you some pamphlets."

She glanced at him sideways.

"Maybe I'd rather learn how to make a shirt like yours?" she said.

"Well, that's possible too," said Michael.

191

"Is that what you mean by an alternative career?"

"You've got it," said Michael. "But spinning and weaving aren't in my field of expertise. You'll have to consult Faith about that. I mainly give advice on farming and animal husbandry. And you don't by any chance happen to know who owns the big house and the surrounding paddocks?"

"It belongs to the British Mining Company," said Helena.

"It's land going to waste that ought to be utilized," said Michael. "This valley is desperately short of agricultural land. If we're to establish any degree of self-sufficiency within the community, we could do with those paddocks."

"I suppose it might be possible to rent them," said Helena. "If you were to get in touch with Sir Gerald Fraser at the company's head office in London . . ."

"How about the outbuildings?" asked Michael.

"The barn's been converted to a billiards room," said Helena. "And the stables are garages. And the dairy's a utility room. They did it all up last winter before we moved in."

"You mean that's where you live?"

"My father's the colliery manager."

Michael rose to his feet.

"I'm sorry," he murmured. "I've made a mistake."

"What mistake?" asked Helena.

"I should have realized before."

"Realized what?"

"We're used to counseling the unemployed, you see?"

"Well, I'm unemployed," said Helena.

"I mean people who have nothing to hope for and nothing to lose," said Michael. "We're into basic human survival. An alternative way of life . . . hard work with no wages attached. A spirit of community with everyone pulling together and making a contribution. How can you possibly fit into that?"

"I have friends in Ynysceiber!" said Helena.

"Maybe you do," said Michael. "But you don't exactly live their kind of life, do you? There's nothing you lack, is there? If you want to set up a riding stable for rich people on vacation . . . then go ahead and do it. Go ahead and enroll in a college course in spinning and weaving. You don't need my help, Helena."

"I see," Helena said bitterly.

And what she saw was another dismissal, another rejection. Michael was refusing to help her because of what she was . . . just as Hugh had refused to go on loving her. It was as if she were some kind of alien species with no feelings, no wants, no needs or desires, not a human being at all. And all they ever thought about was her father's money.

"Maybe I'd like to find another way of living!" Helena said angrily. "Maybe I'd like to live a kind of life that's less offensive to other people. Maybe that's what I want anyway!"

Michael nodded.

"You know what they say . . . it's easier for a camel to enter the eye of a needle than for a rich man . . ."

"Since when have you been Jesus Christ?" asked Helena.

He spread his hands.

"Okay . . . I had no right to say that. I apologize. And of course, if you're ever in the vicinity of the riverside parking lot, you'll be welcome to come in for advice, the same as everyone else."

His politeness hurt, cruel as an insult.

And she watched him walk away down the hillside, the

incident over as far as he was concerned. But Helena was not going to forget. She would visit the alternative-careers advisory service first thing tomorrow morning, just to spite him.

■ ■ ■

There were eight caravans ranged around the parking lot, brightly painted, with colored awnings shading their doorways from the sun. Outside, various members of the alternative-careers advisory team had set up their displays of printed pamphlets, the assorted crafts and artifacts produced by cottage industry. Some gave demonstrations: a bearded man with a treadle lathe turning spindle legs for tables and chairs . . . an elderly woman pounding fragrant herbs with a pestle and mortar, mixing ointments and brewing elderberry linctus on a small camp stove . . . a girl making sun hats out of braided straw . . . another man weaving wattle fence panels and strange conical beehives. A couple of local men watched him and questioned, and younger children made spiral pots out of wet clay.

Hugh sat on the wooden steps of a plum-colored caravan and sipped lemon-balm tea. Again it was their clothing that was most noticeable . . . the patchwork hues, the wonderful jumbled mixtures of soft muted colors. Hanks of fiber, in those same subtle shades, hung on a clothes rail beside him, and a girl named Amy wove it into cloth on a portable loom. It was hemp, she said, an incredibly useful plant although it was illegal to grow it without a license. And the dyes also came from plants . . . from onion skins, bracken roots, mosses, and lichens.

"We use wool and flax as well," Amy said brightly. "Making your own fabrics is a wonderfully satisfying thing to do, and it reduces the dependency on chemically produced materials."

"Hugh's interested in hill farming," said Faith.

"Michael's not back yet," said Amy.

"Is there really any point in waiting?" asked Hugh.

"Of course there is," Amy said warmly.

"Michael will find something for you," said Faith. "I know he will."

And Hugh went on waiting . . . for someone he did not know, who Faith and Amy believed could work miracles and sort out Hugh's life. But it was one thing to dream dreams for the people of Ynysceiber, to work with a community and arrange for training and government grants. Another to rehabilitate a single individual for no particular reason except personal preference. Given the opportunity, how did he know, and how did anyone know, what he really wanted in life?

How did he know what abilities lay within him? Or what kind of work might give him pleasure or delight? All he had ever done was endure . . . the back streets of Cardiff, the Central Station, the garbage dump, the coal face. Unimaginable, almost, a life comprising everything he loved . . . the high hills and Helena and those who had been his friends.

Helena would not want it anyway, he thought, no matter what Michael had to offer. And maybe Dilys and Colin and Flutey had their own different dreams. Apart from Di, there was no love left, and only the hills remained . . . and the ants that scuttled across the cracked asphalt at his feet . . . and someone's shadow.

"Sorry to keep you waiting."

195

Hugh looked up.

He was tall and lean, with a patchwork shirt and brown homespun trousers.

"I'm Michael," said the man.

"Hugh," said Hugh.

"Faith says you're interested in hill farming."

"I might be," said Hugh.

"Alone or with others?"

"That depends," said Hugh.

"Depends on what?" asked Michael.

"On what you have to offer, if anything."

"No," said Michael. "You've got it the wrong way around. That's how it used to be, the basis of discontent . . . people fitting in with other people's arrangements, accepting whatever was going, whatever they were obliged to. This time we'll begin as we aim to go on, with what *you* want."

Hugh stared at him.

"You mean you can fix me up with something either way?"

"Shall we go to my caravan and discuss it?" asked Michael.

"You didn't answer my question," said Hugh.

Michael smiled.

"From the land to the cities . . . from the cities to the land . . . it's the law of prodigality, Hugh, the only recourse left for the human species. We've been anticipating it for years . . . and it's gradually happening. Okay, I may have difficulty placing a couple of hundred people . . . but a couple of dozen is no problem. *Now* shall we go to my caravan and discuss it?"

15

Inside the small cluttered caravan, with an ordinance survey map spread on the table, Hugh was hardly aware of anything else. The untimely darkness was no more than a small pause in the conversation as Michael lit the oil lamps. Flickers of sheet lightning through the windows occasionally added to the brightness, and thunder rumbling around the hills mingled with the rustling of papers. And when the weather finally broke, the hard drumming of rain on the roof could not disturb the intensity of his concentration, although he raised his voice above the sound of it.

"Let's get this straight . . ."

"You want me to recap?" asked Michael.

"In words of one syllable minus the philosophy," said Hugh.

Michael chuckled.

And Hugh listened intently as he talked.

Feelings formed inside him, leaped and twisted. He wanted to laugh, shout, dance, run wild through the streets . . . but still he was compelled to question . . . go through it all again, summing it up, checking and double-checking until he was absolutely sure he understood everything and there was no possible chance he had got things wrong, misinterpreted or made a mistake.

"And this is for real, is it?"

"Subject to confirmation, of course."

"So why weren't we told about it before? Why doesn't everyone know about it? Why's there no information in schools and in the job centers?"

"I told you," said Michael. "It's a gradual thing. We have to find placements, individual landowners willing to cooperate. We simply couldn't handle a mass exodus."

"And you're quite sure about this particular . . ."

"I wouldn't be offering it if I wasn't sure," said Michael.

Hugh nodded.

Then he took one last look at the map he had asked to borrow, folded it carefully and rose to his feet. And the feelings were still inside him, wanting out and needing to be expressed. But his voice stayed steady and he shook Michael's hand.

"I'll see you tomorrow then?"

"I'll look forward to it," Michael replied.

"I'll have to talk it over, see?"

"Take as long as you need. We're here for at least a week."

"And I would like to express my appreciation . . ."

"I'm only doing my job," said Michael.

"Yes," said Hugh. "But thank you anyway."

He turned to go.

"You're going to get soaked," said Michael.

"You could be right about that," said Hugh.

"If you want to wait . . . ?"

"What's a drop of rain on an occasion like this?" Hugh tucked the map down the front of his jeans. "I'll make a run for it," he said.

The rain soaked him the moment he stepped outside . . . drenched his shirt and streamed through his hair. It was warm, heavy, releasing the scents of things . . . the scents of earth and dust and rank vegetation on the riverbank. Even the town smelled sweet and clean, the air pungent with life. And he was a part of it, alive and elated, all the feelings inside him heaving to the surface in huge whoops of joy. He leaped and pranced up the empty street, danced in the water that flowed down the gutters, held his arms wide to embrace the sky. And the rain speared him, slashed at his face, the noise of it drowning his cries.

"D'you hear me, Ynysceiber?

"Are you listening, everyone?

"I'm leaving, see?

"I'm moving on!

"You can shove this town!

"You can shove your jobs!

"There's going to be a vacancy at the colliery!

"And you're welcome to have it!

"I'm leaving!

"Going for good!"

Lightning flickered, made silhouettes of the surrounding hills. And the gray houses huddled beneath them in the semidarkness, wet roofs shining, doors and windows closed against the coming night. He did not know what the time

199

was. He did not care that he should have reported back to the mine. Ynysceiber was over and done with, the rest of his life elsewhere, in another place.

"Llanbach!

"Beloved land!

"Hear that, do you? All of you?

"That's where I'm going!"

He rounded the corner opposite the grocery store. And he was still shouting, still dancing, the map warm and protected against his belly as the rain poured down. He saw Bethesda Street washed clean of everything, all the squalid memories, the hostility and hate. Torrential streams swept down the bank behind the houses, cut tiny channels in the coal-dust hillside and overflowed across the vacant lot. His feet squelched inside his shoes as he rounded the end terrace, opened the gate and paddled across the yard. Potato parings floated in a bucket of water. And when he pressed his face against the kitchen window, someone was staring out at him . . . the dark glitter of eyes and the white gash of a smile.

"Can I come in?" mouthed Hugh.

■ ■ ■

Flutey opened the door before Hugh even reached it. Sinewy arms hauled him inside and closed out the weather. The kitchen smelled of fries and cabbage and vinegar. Rain dripped from his clothes and hair, and his voice was a whisper.

"Where's the others?"

"In the front room," murmured Flutey. "Gwyn and Hacker are in there too. They said you'd torn up those letters. But we were going to return to work next week any-

200

way. Glenda's milk is drying up, and the shops won't give credit, and we need to buy baby food . . ."

"You could have asked. . . ."

"We wanted to, me and Glenda. But the others wouldn't let us. You know how stiff-necked Dilys and Colin can be. And David's as bad. Gwyn and Hacker have managed to talk them around a bit . . ."

"So they won't mind if I . . . ?"

"They're worried," said Flutey.

"Who is?"

"Gwyn and Hacker," said Flutey. "You were supposed to meet them outside the post office, but you weren't there. And when the storm broke, and you hadn't reported back to the colliery, Mr. Boyd telephoned to see if you were with Helena. But she hadn't seen you, and she came down to ask Di, and Di said you hadn't been home for tea, so they came here. They're trying to decide what to do. I mean, it's nearly half past seven and if you'd been out on the hills and got struck by lightning . . ."

"I've been struck by something," said Hugh. "But it wasn't lightning. You wait till I tell you, Flutey! You'll never believe it."

But Flutey headed along the hallway.

And opened the inner door.

"Hugh's here," he announced. "You want me to tell him to push off? Or can he come in?"

There was an awkward silence. And within the room nothing had changed. Hugh saw the bare floorboards, the red-flocked wallpaper on the chimney breast, the threadbare blanket used as a curtain. But *they* were different, their faces wary in the light . . . Colin and David anxiously watching him and waiting for a reaction . . . Glenda cradling Rhiannon

201

in her arms, her hazel eyes quiet and appealing . . . Dilys beside her, regarding him fiercely from the heather sofa on which she normally slept. Only Gwyn and Hacker looked pleased to see him, both of them smiling with relief. But he had no chance to greet them. The uncertainty ended suddenly as Dilys rose from her seat and came leaping toward him. She was all arms and legs and wild red hair, hugging him to her, then thrusting him away.

"It's good to see you, Hugh *bach*."

"You too, *cariad*."

"You're soaked!"

"It's raining, see?"

"And where the hell have you been?"

"That's what I've come to tell you."

"We were about to organize a search party!"

"You know what they say about bad pennies . . . ?"

"So don't just stand there in the doorway," said Dilys. "Come on in and take your clothes off."

Glenda giggled.

"That's not what I meant!" said Dilys.

Then there were movements, a flurry of activity, and everyone talking together. Dilys fetched a towel and Colin's spare sweatshirt. David lent him a pair of trousers. Glenda laughed and kissed him, and Rhiannon cried. Flutey brewed tea and made him a sandwich, and Hacker went to inform Di and Mrs. Di he was home safely. They had to be worrying, said Gwyn.

"Tell them to come and join us," Dilys said gruffly.

"Tell them we're having a reunion party," said Flutey.

"I wish we were," Colin said morosely.

"I suppose we've all been pretty stupid," said David.

"Can't we put it all behind us now?" asked Glenda. "I

mean we're sorry on both sides, aren't we? It's been awful for everyone. So why don't we just forget what's happened and start again?"

"The miners won't forget," said Gwyn.

"But who gained who a reduction in wages?" asked Colin.

"That's got nothing to do with it," said Gwyn.

"Once a scab, always a scab," said David.

"And the grudge will remain for as long as we live in Ynysceiber," said Gwyn.

"You mean all this nastiness is going to go on?" asked Flutey.

"Not between *us*," Dilys said firmly.

"You'd be better off ignoring us," said Gwyn.

"But we don't want to," said Glenda.

"So what'll we do?" asked Flutey.

"Move," muttered Dilys.

"Where?" asked David.

"Anywhere out of Ynysceiber," said Dilys.

"How would we live?"

Dilys shrugged. "Beg? Sell our bodies? Peddle joy drops? Go shoplifting? Or how about sheep rustling? Plenty of sheep, there are, out there on the hills. We could help ourselves, drive them to the nearest market. Or maybe we could organize a bank raid."

"We're not that desperate!" said Colin.

"I am," said Dilys. "I'm finished with this place. I'm sick of hating people I like and I'm sick of being cooped up in this house. There's nothing in Ynysceiber for me, is there? I'm not part of anything, not involved in anything. I feel meaningless, see? I want to *do* something with my life, not be dependent on my brother or some future husband. Nor the bloody welfare either!"

"You ought to try working down the pit!" said Colin.

Rhiannon cried and Glenda rocked her. Rain lashed the window, and the room turned grim as their faces, full of tensions and grievances and an almighty anger that had yet to break. And all the while Hugh had been trying to tell them. There was an alternative to Ynysceiber, an alternative to working in the colliery. Not unemployment and the poverty and degradation that went with it, but something else, an independent future for all of them. He reached for the ordinance survey map and spread it on the floor.

"You want an answer to all your problems?" said Hugh. "Well, here it is, look you."

■ ■ ■

Helena made scrambled egg on toast and took it upstairs to her mother. Then she opened a can of salmon, divided it between two plates, added the last remaining salad ingredients and a hunk of bread and butter and carried the meal through to the dining room for herself and her father. The hall clock chimed a quarter to eight when they seated themselves at the table . . . and it was almost dark outside, rain sluicing against the patio doors, washing away the reflections of the room in runnels of light.

"Is this the best you can do?" asked Mr. Boyd.

"What's wrong with it?" asked Helena.

"It's not exactly imaginative, is it?"

"It's more than a lot of people are having!" Helena retorted.

"Didn't they teach cookery at that school you went to?"

"It was optional," said Helena. "And I chose fashion designing and needlework instead."

She added mayonnaise to the limp lettuce leaves and slices

204

of overripe tomato. The cucumber was soft, and the bread was stale, and without Angharad there was no one to do the shopping. There was no link with Ynysceiber and the outside world either, except for her father.

"Did Hugh turn up?" she asked.

"He hadn't when I left," said Mr. Boyd.

"So where is he then?"

"I'm not responsible for the off-hours activities of the employees, Helena."

"It wasn't off hours when you telephoned, was it? It was only four o'clock. And why wasn't he at work anyway? Surely he didn't just walk out without telling anyone?"

"He was in the town delivering an official circular to the miners," said Mr. Boyd. "I gather he had some kind of fit."

"You mean he was taken ill?"

"No," said Mr. Boyd. "I mean he went berserk . . . flipped his lid or whatever the current expression is . . . tore up the envelopes and threw them in the gutter."

"Why would he do that?"

"Your guess is as good as mine," said Mr. Boyd.

"So what was in them?"

"An official circular. I've already told you that."

"So what did it say?" Helena persisted.

Her father shrugged.

"It was just an ultimatum issued by head office. Either the miners return to work at reduced wages by the end of the week or they lose their jobs."

Helena stared at him.

"That's moral blackmail, Daddy!"

"I'm afraid it's general practice these days, Helena."

"And you went along with it?"

"I wasn't offered a choice," said Mr. Boyd. "If it had been

left up to me, I would simply have waited until the miners returned to work of their own accord. And obviously it's going to make me pretty unpopular, which is why we're being transferred to Yorkshire, of course."

"So what about integrity?" asked Helena.

"What about it?" asked Mr. Boyd.

"Haven't you got any?"

Her father slammed down his knife and fork.

"What did you expect me to do?" he asked bitterly. "Object, and put my own position at risk? Who's going to pay the household bills if I lose my job? Who's going to pay for you to go through university?"

"I don't want to go to university!" Helena said furiously. "I'm not going to end up like you, another shit in the same system! And you're not using me as an excuse for your immoral practices! The miners have little enough to live on as it is without being forced to take a wage cut. And I'm not surprised Hugh flipped his lid! It's a stinking thing to do!"

She threw her napkin on the table.

And rose to her feet.

"I'm going out!" she said.

"Don't be stupid," her father said wearily.

"I no longer wish to be associated—"

"It's pouring with rain, Helena!"

"You can open a can of pineapple for dessert!"

"Will you listen to me!"

"No," said Helena. "Not anymore."

■ ■ ■

The door opened quietly and Di entered the room.

"Where's the reunion party then?"

"Ssh!" said Dilys.

"I've just been down the pub and bought a flagon of cider."

"We'll have it later," said Hacker.

"Planning where to go on next year's vacation, are we?"

"We're just studying the map," said Colin.

"And X marks the spot, does it?"

"Stop interrupting," said Gwyn.

"So what's going on?" asked Di.

"Hugh was just about to tell us," said Glenda.

"Where did I get to?" asked Hugh.

"Llanbach farm," said Flutey.

"Owned by a Mr. Lloyd-Jones," said David, "who is seventy-five years old. His wife died last year, and he suffers from arthritis, and he has no immediate family. His land is being willed to the Powys County Authorities, who offer him the tenancy for life, but who also subcontract to various other tenants on a land-share basis. That right, is it?"

"Yes," said Hugh.

"So what's it got to do with us?"

"Well," said Hugh, "he's getting on a bit, see? Can't manage like he used to. Needs some help, he does, and someone to look after him in old age. There's mountain grazing, about eight acres of walled paddocks, various outbuildings, a three-bedroom farmhouse, and an additional cottage higher up the mountain. It's just ruins at the moment, but we could make it habitable . . ."

"What exactly are you saying?" asked Glenda.

"We can go there," said Hugh. "Whenever we like. Take over the running. Mr. Lloyd-Jones is willing to share the house, although some of us are going to have to rough it for a while . . . until we can repair the cottage or build extra accommodation. If we go for the original Icelandic-type cabins, built into the hill slope and roofed with turf, it shouldn't cost much apart from our labor. And on eight acres of land Michael reckons we can grow enough food for sixteen people . . ."

"Hang on a minute," said Colin.

"Let him finish," said Dilys.

"Where was I?" Hugh asked again.

"Food enough for sixteen people," said Flutey.

"Plus a crop of hemp for winter fuel," said Hugh. "We'll need a license for that. And we'll have to buy milk goats and chickens, seeds and implements and things, but we can claim an agricultural refurbishment grant to cover the initial outlay. And for the first twelve months we get paid one hundred ecu a week each under the Enterprise Allowance Scheme. After that we're on our own. But by then we'll be self-sufficient and beholden to no one . . . except the old man, of course."

He paused for breath.

Rain down the chimney made black splash marks on the tiled hearth. And the others knelt in a semicircle around him, staring at him in openmouthed silence, or gazing at the map spread on the floor before them.

"So what do you think?" asked Hugh.

The silence went on.

"You coming with me, or not?"

"You mean all of us?" asked Hacker.

"You said you wanted to leave Ynysceiber," said Hugh.

"But we don't know anything about farming!" said Colin.

"Mr. Lloyd-Jones does," said Hugh. "And Michael says

208

there are various instructors attached to the alternative-careers service who travel around to various places where they're needed. Obviously we're going to need tuition in some things. We've got to learn to provide for all our basic needs, see?"

"So we'll all be earning a living from one small farm?" asked David. "Including the farmer himself? I don't see how that's possible, Hugh. I mean most small farms went out of business decades ago because they couldn't make a profit."

"You've missed the point," said Gwyn. "It's not about earning a living or making a profit. It's a way of life—people working together, pooling their time and abilities."

"I think it's a wonderful idea," said Dilys.

"It depends what he's like," said Glenda.

"Who?" asked Hugh.

"Mr. Lloyd-Jones."

Hugh sat back on his heels.

"He could be crotchety, cantankerous, set in his ways . . . I don't know what he's like, Glenda *bach*. I only know he's wise enough, or needy enough, to see what has to be and go along with it. It's a slow happening, Michael says. People who cannot survive in the cities are moving back to the land, and those who are owning the land are gradually agreeing to accommodate them. And this old man is one of them. He is relinquishing his ownership and expressing his willingness to share. It's the greatest gift anyone can give . . . a chance of life to a few other people. And I, for one, will not be turning him down. And if he is needing someone to care for him for the rest of his days, then that is what I shall be doing, see? With or without the rest of you."

"I think it's wonderful," Dilys repeated.

Her blue eyes shone, and there was an inane grin on her face . . . the same glee Hugh had felt, waiting to come free. And the room seemed poised, full of questions Hugh did not know about, answers he could not guess. Through the long-drawn-out seconds he sat and waited for someone to speak. And the storm rocked the walls of the house a million miles away in Ynysceiber.

"So when do we leave?" asked Di.

■   ■   ■

Helena pulled up the hood of her duffle coat, tucked the cake tin under her arm and scuttled across the street. Water swilled across the vacant lot, swirled darkly along the gutter, and the rain slanted golden beneath streetlights. The back-yard was awash, and her boots made a tide that swilled against the walls and lapped at the doorstep. She knocked, twice, but no one heard her. Then she tried the handle and let herself in.

It was dark inside the kitchen, full of stale food smells, and just for a moment she could not remember the way. Then above the noise of the rain she heard voices and laughter, and groped her way along the hall. They were having a reunion party, Mrs. Di had told her, and a line of light showed beneath the door to the front room. Helena hesitated, aware that she was an intruder in someone else's home, a gate crasher who had not been invited.

"Hugh?" she called.

Again no one answered.

Their laughter grew louder.

And upstairs the baby began to cry.

Helena opened the door.

It was a strange scene. The room was uncarpeted and bare of furniture . . . just the pile of heather on the floor in one corner, someone's bed with a couple of torn sheets for covers . . . the ghastly red-flocked paper on the wall above the hearth, and the blanket nailed across the window instead of curtains. And they took turns drinking cider from a bottle, all of them laughing and cheering and capering about . . . Hugh and Dilys doing a crazy dance with a couple of young men Helena did not know . . . and Flutey wiping tears from his eyes. No one noticed Helena standing in the doorway. No one included her . . . until Glenda happened to turn her head.

"Helena?"

Their movements ceased.

And the silence was electrifying.

Helena removed her hood.

"I couldn't make anyone hear," she said lamely.

"Come on in," said Dilys.

"Join the party," said Glenda.

"This is Hacker . . . and this is Gwyn," said Dilys.

Helena looked at Hugh.

"Mrs. Di said you were here."

"She must be wondering where I've got to," said Di.

"She's made a cake to celebrate," said Helena. "She says she'll be over as soon as she's finished the dishes. In about five minutes, she said." She gave the tin to Flutey. "It's a chocolate sponge," she told him.

"I'll go and put it in the kitchen," said Flutey.

"And I'll go and get some more cider," said Di.

"I'll give you a hand," said Colin.

"And we really ought to be going," said Gwyn.

"You don't have to," said Helena. "Not because of me."

"Aren't you Mr. Boyd's daughter?" asked Hacker.

"He told me what happened this afternoon," said Helena.

"Yes," Hacker said curtly. "Well, it's nice to have met you."

The room slowly emptied.

Upstairs Rhiannon was crying.

Hungry, said Glenda, and they had nothing to feed her.

Except sponge cake, said Dilys.

Which was worth a try, said David.

"I'll see you in a minute," Dilys said to Helena.

And then only Hugh remained.

And the ordinance survey map spread on the floor.

"I didn't mean to break things up," said Helena.

"You haven't," said Hugh.

"I just wanted to know if you were all right."

"You needn't have worried . . ."

"I just wanted to know, that's all. And I'm glad you're all friends again."

"Yes," said Hugh.

"I was hoping you and I could . . . ? I mean I'm not expecting anything, but . . ."

Hugh shook his head.

"We're going," he said.

"Going?" said Helena. "How do you mean?"

"We're leaving Ynysceiber," said Hugh.

"All of you?"

"Yes."

Desperate feelings lurched inside her.

"When?" she asked.

"Sunday?" said Hugh.

"This coming Sunday?"

"Or maybe Monday. It depends on the weather."

Her desperation grew.

"You can't!" she said. "What about your job? I know it's not well paid, but it's better than nothing! You can't just chuck everything in and leave! It doesn't make sense!"

"I'm sorry," said Hugh. "But a job isn't the answer, not anymore. We've got to find some kind of alternative existence, a different way of life, learn to be self-sufficient . . ."

"You've been talking to Michael, haven't you?"

"You've met him?"

"I met him," Helena said bitterly.

"He's fixed us up with something, see?"

"Where?"

"A place called Llanbach," said Hugh.

"That's a farm, I suppose?"

"Out in the mountains, the Brecon Beacons," said Hugh.

"I see."

Her voice was bleak. And her feelings tore at her, cruel and hurting. There had been endings before between her and Hugh, but not like this one . . . final, irrevocable, offering no hope of reconciliation. This time there would be forty or fifty miles of distance between them. He would go away and live his life without her and she would never see him again. The room blurred with her tears.

"I hope you'll be very happy, Hugh."

"I'm sorry, Helena."

She turned away from him.

Her footsteps echoed along the hallway. Rhiannon

213

screamed, and David came from the kitchen with a finger of sponge cake on a plate. He spoke her name, but she shook her head dumbly, pushed past Dilys and Flutey, who were in the kitchen, and let herself out into the night. The kind wild darkness surrounded her, and the tears on her face were indistinguishable from the rain.

16

Dawn streaked the eastern sky with tinges of pink above the opposite hills, although the mist was rising in the valley below. And they left silently . . . with Rhiannon's cradle reverted back to a handcart, laden with essential belongings and trundling through the sleeping streets. Sidewalks glistened with damp. Doors and windows and For Sale signs were running with moisture. Their footsteps seemed muffled as the mist swirled around them, and when they arrived at the post office, there was no sign of Gwyn and Hacker. They waited and their feet and hands grew chill, the children restless with the delay.

"Where *is* Gwyn and Hacker anyway?" demanded William.

"*Are,*" said Mrs. Di.

"And why do we have to wait for them?" asked Olwen.

"They're supposed to be coming with us," said Glenda.

"Maybe they've got cold feet?" said Flutey.

"So have I," said William.

"Gwyn wouldn't let us down," said Dilys.

"We could walk on slowly," suggested David.

"And hope they'll catch up with us," said Colin.

"Well, it's up to them," said Di.

They continued on down the street . . . past the second-hand clothes shop with nothing in it . . . past the welfare office and the employment center that offered no vacancies . . . past the parking lot where the caravans of the alternative-careers service were based . . . over the river bridge and across the railway line to join the main road from Cardiff. There a divided highway led out of Ynysceiber and headed toward the now invisible hills. Neath and Merthyr, the rusting road signs said.

They waited again, then walked slowly up the long hill, but Gwyn and Hacker failed to catch up with them. And their absence affected them, blighted their mood. They were silent as a funeral procession . . . Rhiannon sleeping in a sling against Glenda's chest, and Di's children walking demurely beside their mother, Di carrying the family suitcase, and David with a travel bag, a shopping bag full of baby things and the guitar strung around his neck. Colin and Flutey puffed and sweated as they shoved the handcart. And even Dilys had nothing to say.

And it was not just Gwyn and Hacker being left behind, thought Hugh, but Helena, too, and Ynysceiber itself . . . all that had happened there, the joy and the sadness, the summer heat and the few crammed months of their lives. And what lay ahead of them was all unknown, an old man and an unimaginable life, the powers of a land none of them knew how to manage. It was a frightening prospect, almost a kind of dying. They were turning their backs on the whole structure of human society and relying only on each other, knowing that any or even all of them could fail or fall short, cave in under their own weaknesses or let the others down, as Gwyn and Hacker already had.

They had their reasons, he supposed, jobs in the colliery and their own particular fears. Not easy to relinquish what security they had for a bunch of outsiders and a dream that was not their own. Between theory and practice there was too much finality. And he was depressingly aware of his own shortcomings, the fragility of human relationships, and the enormous changes required to make things work.

Then, momentarily, his spirits lifted. The mist cleared and the distances opened out . . . endless miles of dead grass, gorse and heather, devoid of human habitation . . . and the road curving away around a flank of the hillside toward the cloudless sky. And when he turned to look back, Ynysceiber was gone, the colliery and the valley and the world beyond it vanished as if they had never been. And the hills floating like islands in an ocean of whiteness that went on as far as he could see.

"We're really on our own now, aren't we?" said David.

"As if the whole human race has been wiped out," said Colin.

"Except for Highview House," said Flutey.

Hugh could see it, tiny among the distant trees. Helena, lost to him forever, unreachable on another island in the same sea of cloud. It was almost symbolic. And the lump in his throat threatened to choke him. He heard the others leaving, heard the handcart rattle on up the hill, but all he could feel was an overwhelming grief that seemed to root him to the spot.

217

"I know how you feel," Dilys said softly.

"Do you?" said Hugh.

"I really liked Gwyn, see? Well, I liked Hacker too."

"I'm sorry," said Hugh. "I didn't know."

"Yes," said Dilys. "And it hurts, see? And that's the same for both of us. And there was never any hope for you and Helena, but Gwyn was coming with us and we'd made plans . . ." She dashed a hand across her eyes. "Well, at least you're not by yourself," she said. "And you do have the consolation of knowing you did right by Helena. It was much kinder to let her go."

"I bet she didn't see it like that."

"But she couldn't possibly have come with us, could she?"

"I suppose not," sighed Hugh.

"It's just not her kind of life, see?"

"I could have given her the chance, though."

Dilys shook her head.

"Suppose you had persuaded her? What then? She would never have coped. We're going to be roughing it all through the winter, working and living in mud and muck and God knows what. Helena would hate it and you would be hating yourself for exposing her to it. Best as it is, Hugh. And no need for you to feel sorry."

"I can't help what I feel, Dilys."

"Well, it's no good standing here brooding, is it?"

"Maybe we grieve in different ways?" said Hugh.

"There's a new life ahead of us, Hugh."

"I'll catch up with you," he told her.

She shrugged and left him, went running after the others, shouting at them to wait. And Hugh felt the spaces growing, heard their footsteps fading and others coming toward him.

Or maybe he only imagined someone approaching and the soft rattle of wheels? He turned to look. The wall of mist was receding down the road to Ynysceiber, and he could see shapes within it . . . rocks and gorse bushes and a nearby fence post, and a gray human form dragging something behind it.

■　■　■

On Sunday morning Helena rose as the sun rose over the opposite hills, dressed in jeans and a sweater, and crept downstairs lugging the heavy suitcase. She had written a note to her parents the previous evening, and propped it against the toaster for them to find. She made sandwiches for the journey, mayonnaise and tuna fish, and stowed them in her shoulder bag with a bag of cookies, two apples and a bottle of mineral water. Then she put on her duffle coat and left by the back door.

Her footsteps crunched on the gravel, a loud intrusive sound. And the gate rattled when she opened it. Her heart thumped nervously as she deposited her keys in the box, but no one heard, no one came after her. She breathed a sigh of relief and hurried down the lane, towing the suitcase behind her. Dead grass and gorse were laced with cobwebs and raindrops, shimmering in the sunlight, but the valley below was hidden in a sea of fog.

The lane led into it, and the air grew chill, and all she could see were the vague gray shapes of the houses. She walked determinedly along Bethesda Street, unsure of her welcome but willing to argue with them anyway, willing to fight for her life. But the blanket was gone from the front-room window of the end terrace, and opposite Mrs. Di had taken down her curtains. When Helena pressed her face to the glass, she saw a few remaining items of furniture that were impossible to carry, but nothing else.

Blind panic gripped her. They had left already . . . and she had no way of knowing when. But they would not have gone yesterday, she reasoned. Yesterday it had rained. So they must have left this morning . . . an hour ago, or half an hour ago, or maybe only minutes before Helena arrived. Maybe if she hurried she could catch up with them. Unless she went home? Tore up the letter to her parents? Forgot about Hugh, and Faith, and the plum-colored caravan, all the plans she had made and the dreams that had grown in her mind? But it was not for Hugh she had made her decision, not for him she needed to create some purpose in her life, but for herself. And if she gave up now, in a moment of fear or anxiety, she might never have another opportunity.

Heedless of the noise she made, Helena turned and ran, the suitcase careering after her, clattering on its wheels. Three days she had spent studying and researching everything that might be involved . . . visiting the alternative-careers advisory service and talking things over. She had gathered names of contacts and sources of supplies, made surreptitious telephone calls and crammed her mind with information. She was not going ignorant and useless into some unknown venture. She was primed and ready for all eventualities.

Unseen in the mist, she ran across the bridge and headed up the divided highway toward Neath, the route she had memorized from her father's road atlas becoming reality. She was hot and sweating in her boots and duffle coat, and the case grew heavier as she hauled it up the incline, but she would not stop. Then the mist grew golden with sunlight and began to thin, and she saw someone standing on the roadway ahead of her. He was indistinct at first but grew clearer as Helena approached . . . a long-haired youth in a maroon-and-blue track suit with her father's tweed jacket on top.

Helena slowed and stopped.

Her suitcase toppled.

And her breath came in short hard gasps.

"Helena?" Hugh stared at her, as if he could not believe she was real. "What the hell are you doing here?"

"I'm coming with you," said Helena. "To Llanbach farm."

Hugh shook his head in bewilderment.

"You've got to be crazy!"

"And you're not?"

"It's different for us."

"Why is it different?"

"Because we've got nothing to lose."

"Nor have I," said Helena. "Not anymore."

"What about your parents?"

"I left them a note," said Helena.

"That's not what I meant."

"It's my life, Hugh."

"And have you any idea of what you're going to? Any conception of what it might be like? It's no picnic, girlie!"

"I'll pull my weight," Helena assured him.

"You really think you're cut out for this kind of life?"

"I don't see why not," said Helena. "I'm as fit as anyone else. And how do I know what I'm cut out for until I try? I may have been born with a silver spoon in my mouth, but I can work as hard as the next person if the need arises. And I've talked to Faith, so I know what I'm doing. But if you don't want me . . ."

221

"That's not it."

"So why are we arguing?"

"You can't just give up everything . . ."

"I'm not," said Helena. "I'm not giving up anything, can't you see that? I've brought it all with me . . . my clothes and my savings book . . . and what else is there? Everything else belongs to my parents and the British Mining Company. This is all I have, Hugh, and all I am . . . just myself. Isn't it enough?"

"You're going to find it terribly hard, Helena."

"And you won't?" she inquired.

He ran out of arguments.

Stared at her helplessly.

And spread his hands.

"I'm not going to ask you," he said.

Helena smiled.

"No," she said. "I didn't expect you to. This is my decision, Hugh. Whatever happens is my responsibility and nothing to do with you. Is that all right?"

Hugh laughed.

The early-morning sunlight glittered around them.

And the world seemed golden.

"You're amazing," he said.

"You haven't seen anything yet," said Helena. "You've no idea how truly amazing I am. I can't believe it myself, really. Now hadn't we better go before the others wonder where you are?"

She hauled her suitcase on along the road.

And left him standing.

And a few moments later he came hurrying after her.

"Carry your bags, miss?"

"Thanks," said Helena. "But I've already told you . . .

I'll pull my own weight. Let's start as we mean to go on, shall we?"

■ ■ ■

The others were waiting as Hugh and Helena rounded the bend, sitting together on an outcrop of rocks beside the road. And what they thought and felt about her joining them was clear behind their smiles, behind their eyes. They were as doubtful as Hugh had been, thinking she was probably not even up to a twenty-five-mile hike, let alone life on a Welsh hill farm. But she offered no explanation for her presence, just stripped off her duffle coat, sat on a boulder between Di and Mrs. Di, drank a mouthful of mineral water, and made no complaint when, two minutes later, they decided to move on.

"Know where you're going, do you?" Colin asked her.

"First turning right past Merthyr Tydfil," Helena retorted.

"Which is more than you knew," said Glenda.

"The girl's all right," Di said admiringly.

"But if you'd had any sense you'd have swiped your Da's Mercedes and given us a lift!" said Dilys.

"Maybe I'll give you a lift anyway," said Helena.

"You and whose army?" asked David.

"You wait and see," Helena said mysteriously.

There was a certainty about her Hugh had never noticed before, a kind of power . . . a spring in her step, a flush on her face, an excitement in her eyes. It was as if something within her had come alive, as if she had found a purpose. She dragged the suitcase as if it were weightless, and he toiled behind, shoving the handcart, watching the wind chase the strands of her hair, listening to her voice, the ban-

223

ter of renewed friendships. It was true what she had said . . . she was there not for him but for herself. The echoes of her laughter drew farther and farther ahead, and she seemed not to care whether he was following or not.

Then he forgot her. The handcart hit a pothole in the road, tipped and shed its load before he could right it. Sauce-pans rolled and clattered. Mugs and plates smashed. Socks and underpants spilled from Flutey's bag. And when he finally reached the head of the valley where the road divided, Helena was no longer with them. Her suitcase was there, dumped on the grass, but she was small in the distance and heading away along the road to Neath.

"What have you been saying to her?" he demanded.

"Nothing," said Dilys.

"She just upped and left us," said Colin.

"Said she was going to visit someone," said David.

"And she said not to wait for her," said Flutey. "She'd catch up with us on the road, she said. But we can't very well go on without her, can we?"

"And we can't hang about here all day either," said Colin. "Not if we're hoping to reach Llanbach before dark. And if we don't get there before dark, we're not likely to find it, are we? We'll be spending the night in the open! And what happens if it rains? We got the baby to think of, haven't we? And it's *her* flipping fault!"

"Give the girl a chance," said Di.

"She did say she wouldn't be long," said David.

"We can spare half an hour, can't we?" said Flutey.

"And I'm hungry!" William announced.

"I think Rhiannon is, too," said Glenda.

"In that case we'll have an early lunch," said Mrs. Di.

"Postpone the decision, see? Pass me the sandwiches, Olwen."

Hugh sat on the grass. The sun had burned away the morning mist, and the view was clear now all the way down the valley . . . the dark scar of the colliery, the gray smudge that was Ynysceiber. It was clear behind him, too, and on either side in both directions . . . an empty road marching uphill and down across a landscape of moors and bogs and uninhabited wilderness. And Helena headed into it, for some unknown reason. Whatever happened was her responsibility, she had said. But in the minds of the others Hugh was responsible too.

"Whose idea was it for her to come with us?" asked Colin.

"Hers," said Hugh.

"I bet you didn't try to dissuade her either," said Dilys.

"What Helena does is up to her, see?"

"Not when it affects us," said Dilys.

"You're objecting then, are you?"

"We should at least have been consulted!" said Colin.

"It's not that we don't like her," Glenda said gently.

"It's just that she's not likely to be of any use," said David. "I mean she's hardly cut out for this kind of life, is she?"

"And we can't afford to carry passengers," said Dilys.

"Maybe she'll end up carrying you!" Hugh retorted.

"She's nothing but a flipping ornament!" said Dilys.

"She's knocked spots off Gwyn and Hacker," said Mrs. Di.

"What do you mean?" Dilys asked angrily.

"Come farther than they have, hasn't she? And given up her posh life to do so."

"She's got spunk," said Di. "I'll say that for her. And she's not daft neither. She must know well enough what she's heading into. And if she doesn't like it, she can always go home, see?"

"You're saying we should accept her?" asked David.

"Put up with her, more like," said Colin.

"Now there's magnanimous," said Hugh. "How about her putting up with you, boy?"

"Don't let's quarrel," begged Glenda.

"No," said Flutey. "Not now we're all friends again."

"And we do *like* Helena," said Glenda.

Dilys rose to her feet.

"Right!" she said. "That's fine by me. So let's get on with it, shall we? We were told not to wait, remember? And there's a long way to go." She maneuvered the handcart into the road. "Who's going to carry the excess baggage?" she inquired.

■   ■   ■

It was wonderful, thought Helena, everything she felt and the vast empty spaces around her. She loved the speed, and the wind through her hair, sunlight over the hills and the shadows of clouds drifting across the land. She loved the colors of things: the dry oatmeal grasses, the lichen on the rocks, bracken turning orange, and the purple tinge of heather. She wanted to work with colors like that, hemp and wool in natural dyes, make clothes, and curtains, carpets and bedspreads, covers for furniture . . . sheepskin coats, gloves and moccasins and hats. Human hands could create greater beauty than any machine, Faith had said. All Helena needed was a spindle, a loom and a treadle sewing machine.

Llanbach, thought Helena.

226

Llanbach was a lovely name.

And she would help make it a lovely place.

She would have a garden full of herbs and roses and fill the house with their scents. She would keep bees, have honey, make wax polish for the furniture. She would white-wash the inside walls. And who among them, apart from her, had any experience of a life that was not ugly? Who else had lived as she had, could dream as she dreamed and make it real?

And yes, she would have to till the earth, and weed and hoe and spread the manure. And yes, she would have to soil her hands and harden her heart, learn to skin a sheep and gut it when it died, boil the fleece to remove the lanolin, and card the wool until her fingers bled. She would have to flay hemp, cook and clean and carry, do what everyone else did in all winds and weathers, and not complain however sick or tired or fed up she felt. And she would do all that because she, out of all of them, was the only one who had ever been free to do otherwise, the only one who had any real choice.

The others would probably never understand, she thought. They would never understand the elation she felt, the joy of knowing her own usefulness, all she could add to their lives and all she could give. They probably thought she was useless, that she would not be able to do anything and would not even try. They probably thought she would be a burden on them all, a person who was totally incapable. She laughed aloud, anticipating the look on their faces. And the horse trotted on, docile, unflappable, pulling the cart in which she traveled . . . until she hauled on the reins and he stopped.

"Can I give you a lift?" she asked.

Hugh was standing by the roadside.

He was grinning stupidly.

"So that's where you've been!"

"His name's Jimbo," said Helena.

"Jimbo," said Hugh.

And he stroked the shaggy brown mane.

"I ordered him over the telephone," said Helena. "I was going to stay there and work if you hadn't let me come with you. The farm breeds and trains pit ponies, you see? That's what Jimbo was destined to be, but I'm sure he'll have a much better life with us. And we're going to need a horse."

"How much did he cost?" asked Hugh.

"What's that got to do with you?" asked Helena. "It's my money and I'll spend it how I see fit for as long as it lasts. The cart's made from recycled materials. The wheels and chassis and axles come from an old car. Good, isn't it?"

"I won't ask how much that cost," said Hugh.

"Quite right," said Helena. "Why don't you just hop on board and we'll go and pick up the others?"

He heaved her suitcase into the back.

And climbed in beside her.

"Do you want to drive?" Helena asked him.

"I wouldn't know how," said Hugh.

Deftly, she flicked the reins and Jimbo trotted on along the road, the cart bowling smoothly behind him.

"We need a horse," she repeated. "The nearest school is three miles away . . . too far for William and Olwen to walk. And we'll need to fetch supplies from Brecon and take our produce to the market there. Jimbo's our transport. And he'll pull a plow too. I mean we're not likely to be going in for strip farming if we've got paddocked fields. It'll have to be rotational crop growing, won't it?"

She glanced at Hugh.

Saw the disconcerted look on his face.

"Been doing your homework, haven't you?"

"It pays to be prepared," said Helena.

"What else do you know that I don't?"

Helena shrugged.

"I know what Mr. Lloyd-Jones is like and how long he's lived at Llanbach. It belonged to his wife's family until he married her. He's a nice old man, according to the lady who runs the post office shop in Capel How. I telephoned her yesterday. She'll have groceries ready for us to collect and milk for the baby. The house faces west across the valley, she says, and there's a solid-fuel heater in the lean-to for heating water."

"Anything else?" asked Hugh.

Helena shrugged again.

"I know how many potatoes to plant per acre, and what time of year to plant corn and hemp. I know where to apply for the license, and where to order seeds. Faith told me that. Did you know . . . you can not only make cloth from hemp, but rope as well, and paper, and use it for fuel? We'll have to plant trees, of course, but they're for the future. Whereas hemp will mature in a single season." She glanced at him again. "What's the matter?"

"Do *we* get any say in anything?" he asked.

"So what have *you* been doing in the last few days?" Helena asked him.

"Sat on our butts compared to you," said Hugh.

"And whose fault's that?" asked Helena.

He laughed . . . and so did she. And the wind from the

229

mountains carried their laughter away, glad human sounds being scattered over the hills and valleys. And Llanbach was ahead of them . . . life on the land and a group of people walking toward it. Helena tugged at the reins and slowed Jimbo's pace.

"I'm sorry," she said. "I guess I got carried away."

Hugh shook his head.

"Seems you're about to carry us all away, *cariad*."